31 Nights of Halloween

Edited by
Lyle Perez-Tinics

The characters depicted in these short stories are completely fictitious, and any similarities to actual events, locations or people, living or dead, are entirely coincidental.

No part of this publication may be reproduced, in whole or in part, without written permission from the publisher, except for brief quotations in reviews. For information regarding permissions please contact the publisher Contact@RainstormPress.com

ISBN 10 – 0615530826
ISBN 13 – 978-0-61553-0826

31 Nights of Halloween

Rainstorm Press http://www.RainstormPress.com
Copyright © 2011 by Rainstorm Press
All rights reserved

Interior book design by –
The Mad Formatter
www.TheMadFormatter.com

Cover illustration by Lindsay Bobroski
Contact by email: LindsayBabroski@aol.com

Dedicated to the Halloween kid in all of us.

Happy Halloween!

Table of Contents

1st Night: A Pity Party of Monstrous Proportions
By Patrick Shand . . . . Pg 11

2nd Night: Middleton's Gym
By Terry Alexander . . . . Pg 14

3rd Night: Four Nights
By Rebecca Carter . . . . Pg 17

4th Night: Candy Ban
By Maurice Vaughan . . . . Pg 19

5th Night: A Night's Work
By Diandra Linnemann . . . . Pg 22

6th Night: Zombies Don't Trick or Treat
By Rusty Fischer . . . . Pg 27

7th Night: Driving Alone
By Jimalyn Lawless . . . . Pg 29

8th Night: The Spell
By Lyle Perez-Tinics . . . . Pg 31

9th Night: Lights Out
Kevin Walsh . . . . Pg 34

10Th Night: Lorelie
By J. Rodimus Fowler . . . . Pg 39

11th Night: Wretched
By R. M. Cochran . . . . Pg 43

12th Night: Peter, Peter Pumpkin Eater
By S.J. Caunt . . . . Pg 46

13th Night: The Journey Home
By Shawn M. Riddle . . . . Pg 50

14th Night: The Bully Minder
By S. S. Michaels . . . . Pg 54

15th Night: Something is Out there
By Nathan Correll . . . . Pg 57

16th Night: The Licked Hand
By Mark Goddard . . . . Pg 61

17Th Night: Chewy Ones
By Jeff Szpirglas . . . . Pg 65

18Th Night: The Initiation
By Michael C. Dick . . . . Pg 70

19th Night: The Life and Loss of Miss Elizibeth Prince
By J. Rodimus Fowler . . . . Pg 74

20th Night: The Ghost of Gertrude Garvey
By Patrick Shand . . . . Pg 78

21st Night: The Heart Fixer
By Rhiannon Mills . . . . Pg 80

22nd Night: Equinox
By Geoffery Crescent . . . . Pg 84

23rd Night: Trick or Cheat
By Rebecca Snow . . . . Pg 88

24th Night: Bets Beware
By L.J. Landstrom . . . . Pg 92

25th Night: The Damned
By Shawn M. Riddle . . . . Pg 97

26th Night: In a Cat's Eye
By Louise Herring-Jones . . . . Pg 101

27th Night: The Full Moon
By Stuart Conover . . . . Pg 105

28th Night: Check Your Candy
By Eloise J. Knapp . . . . Pg 109

29th Night: Lighthouse
By Benny Alano . . . . Pg 112

30th Night: Bloody Bones
By Diandra Linnemann . . . . Pg 114

31st Night: Wail
By Kate Jonez . . . . Pg 118

Bonus Stories

In the Dead House
By S. S. Michaels . . . . Pg 121

The Monster Under my Bed
By Bryan Medof . . . . Pg 124

Thirteen
By Joe DiBuduo & Kate Robinson . . . . Pg 127

31 Nights of Halloween

A Pity Party of Monstrous Proportions
By Patrick Shand

Zombies, vampires, and werewolves. They marched down the street together, laughing, howling, or groaning *brains*[1] while a strange duo watched the macabre procession from the shadows[2]. One of the watchers was a hulking brute of a man called Frankenstein's Monster[3], and the other was a rather old gentleman wrapped in yellowed strips of gauze. He was known simply as The Mummy. You may have heard of them.

On this particular evening, they were doing what they always did on Halloween: being complete sourpusses. Frankenstein's Monster scowled at the group of monsters and kids walking down the street together, enjoying the holiday that had once been the duo's favorite[4].

"I don't know what it is with these kids," Frankenstein's Monster said, tinkering with one of the bolts that protruded from his temple. "It's as if we never existed! When's the last time you saw a mummy out there, The Mummy?"

"Or a Frankenstein."

"Frankenstein's *monster*," Frankenstein's Monster corrected[5]. The Mummy rolled his eyes but, because they had long since rotted and resembled small brown raisins, Frankenstein's Monster didn't notice.

"It just isn't our holiday anymore, man," The Mummy said, scratching at the hole that had long ago been his prominent nose. "We're not scary to them."

"No, that's the problem," Frankenstein's Monster said, sneering at a group of shirtless, muscular boys that strode past, winking at a pair of zombie girls. "For some reason, it's either sexy vampires or rotty zombies. That's it! Creativity is out the window. I mean, those male model guys are supposed to be werewolves, right? Where's the fur? Not even a snout?"

"Hey, look, there's Dracula," The Mummy said, pointing at a caped fellow with a dramatic widow's peak. On each of the vampire's arms was a young girl with dramatic eye shadow, pale skin, and shirts that read TEAM VAMPIRES ARE HOT[6].

"I bet he's in his glory right now, the jerk," Frankenstein's monster said. "Hey, you want to go teepee his house?"

Before the mummy could respond, Dracula turned to them, his eyes glowing red.

"Damn super hearing," The Mummy said, cursing under his breath in Egyptian.

"Mansion," Dracula said, squeezing the girls closer. "I live in a *mansion*, not a house."

With that, Dracula walked away, his hands dangerously close to the girls' backsides.

"Man," Frankenstein said. "I hate that guy."

The two of them continued watching and sulking until the sun came up. Then, they went inside, watched *Frankenstein* and *The Mummy*, and felt very sorry for themselves.

The End [7]

Footnotes

1. Depending on which they were, of course.
2. Really not as menacing as it sounds. They were under the shadow of a cherry tree, enjoying a pair of non-alcoholic strawberry daiquiris.
3. That is his full name. On the birth certificate and everything.
4. The kids were, of course, unaware that there were true monsters in their numbers. Creatures of the night like to play this trick on Halloween, though it is looked down upon when monsters use this technique to trap and eat children. Punishment for such a crime is ten sharp slaps to the wrist (or tentacle) with the femur of the victim.
5. Frankenstein's Monster has been reminding people for years that Frankenstein himself is merely the *creator* of the monster, failing to realize that no one has ever cared either way.
6. These shirts once bore the name of a specific vampire, a pasty fellow I believe was named Edmund, but these girls decided that *all* undead creatures are sexually attractive, and it would be unfair to pick just one.
7. Unless, of course, Frankenstein's Monster and The Mummy become popular once again. [8]

8. Clearly... The End.

PATRICK SHAND *is just like Romulus and Remus. Except instead of being raised by ravenous yet friendly wolves, he was raised by books. And also parents. After he read all of the books, comics, and plays ever published (it's true, don't worry), he went on a quest to expand his horizons and write his own material. He has written comics such as Joss Whedon's ANGEL and Spike TV's 1000 WAYS TO DIE, in addition to plays that have been produced in NYC and stories that have been included in anthologies and literary magazines. You can read more about him at patrickshand.blogspot.com*

Middleton's Gym
By Terry Alexander

"You won't do it, you don't have the nerve." The thin teenager ran his fingers through his short curly red hair. "No one has ever spent the night there."

"You want to back up that talk with a little wager?" A short pimply-faced boy challenged.

"Just name the amount and I'll match it." The red head nodded.

That's how it started, a stupid bet between two former childhood friends, turned bitter rivals. Twenty bucks to spend the night in the abandoned Carl Middleton High School gym. Sleeping under the same basketball goal where Principal Bill Hinton hanged himself on the final day of school in 1965, when state budget woes and politics closed the grand old facility.

Tom Donovan and Bobby 'Curly' James grew up in the same neighborhood, inseparable as children. They spent each summer together, playing baseball in Cecil Parkers field, and fishing at Lawson's Creek. Things changed, and over time they grew apart, now they craved the affection of the same girl, Karen Matthews, the prettiest girl in their senior class. Her perfect smile and black hair set Tom's heart skipping each time he looked at her.

The date was set for Halloween night at 7:00 o'clock. Since Curly's dad was appointed custodian for the old buildings, his job was to get the key. A chill wind blew on the fateful evening. Several of his classmates escorted him to the Middleton School. Tom told his parents he was spending the night with a friend. His Dad went to Middleton and knew the stories well. He would have a fit if he knew his son's plans.

Tom fumed at the sight of Karen clutching Curly's arm, as they walked into the old gymnasium. The teens toured the old building, admiring the dust covered trophies earned by former students, paying special attention to the basketball goal where Principal Hinton ended his life.

"That's it, huh?" Curly gawked at the iron rim, the brittle net hanging in tatters. "I wonder why Hinton did it, why did he kill himself?"

"When they closed the school, he didn't have anything left to live for." Karen snuggled closer to Curly's side. "It's really sad, but this school was his whole life."

A knife of jealousy twisted in Tom's belly. "You seem to know a lot about it," he said.

"My Grandmother Ruth was Principal Hinton's secretary. She really thought a lot of the man. She still talks about him sometimes." A solemn look creased her face.

The gang left after midnight, leaving Tom alone with his thoughts. Moonlight glowed through the windows, casting irregular elongated patterns on the floor. A series of pops and creaks sent shivers running up the teenager's spine.

"The old girl's just settling." Tom ran a quivering hand through his brown hair.

A stiff wind howled outside, the moon disappeared behind swiftly moving dark clouds. Lightning lit up the sky, scattered raindrops splattered the dust covered windows. Powerful gusts found the cracks and crevices and set the nets swaying. The heavens opened and rain pounded the roof, finding the small openings and dripping inside the building. Heavy footsteps rang on the concrete sidewalk, loud, deliberate footfalls. *It's Curly, he's trying to scare me, make me look bad in Karen's eyes.* The footsteps paused outside the doorway.

The flesh prickled along Tom's arms. The oversized knob turned slowly, the door creaked open on rusty hinges. A man sized shape stood framed in the doorway, tall and reed-like, his nearly transparent form shifting and oozing. Principal Bill Hinton stepped through the threshold, a frayed rope draped around his neck. His shrunken hollow eyes fastened on the basketball goal. Hinton's hard soled shoes banged on the wood floor at every step, the echo carried through the cavernous structure.

Chills raced up his spine, Tom crawled toward the bleachers, circling behind the spirit. *My God, it's real, Hinton's ghost is real.* His sneakers squealed across a rain slick puddle.

Hinton turned at the commotion, moving in a stiff jerky motion. His soulless gaze fastened on the teenager. Thin dead lips stretched back in the mockery of a grin, displaying decayed rotten teeth.

Tom jumped to his feet, and ran to the door. "Let me out," he screamed. "Curly, let me out. You win, do you hear me? You win.

Let me out!" His hand circled the knob. It turned freely in his hand making several complete rotations. He pulled with all his strength, it wouldn't budge. Tom lowered his shoulder and butted the door, it remained tight.

"Curly!" Tom kicked at the door. "Let me out!" His fists pounded on the thick wood, skin peeled away from his knuckles leaving red spots on the peeling paint. "Let me out!" The door wouldn't budge no matter what Tom tried, it refused to move. He stood on tip-toes peering through the upper glass. The door was locked, padlocked from the outside.

"Curly, let me out," he screamed. The loud echo of Hinton's hard soled shoes drew nearer.

Terry Alexander *and his wife Phyllis live on a small farm near Porum, Oklahoma. They have three children and nine grandchildren. Terry is a member of the Oklahoma Writers Federation, Arkansas Ridge Writers, Ozark Writers League and The Fictioneers. He has been published in anthologies from Living Dead Press, Static Movement, Moonstone Books, Paper Cut Publishing, Shade City Press and Knightwatch Press.*

Four Nights
By Rebecca Carter

Halloween night came and she was sure that it was almost over. She had let her imagination run wild and now Jennah was suffering for it. She told herself over and over again that the bumps and clangs in the night were normal-the only reason she didn't notice it before was because there had never been this much silence with all of her roommates here. Jennah never cared much for ghost stories so when her friends all went away for a weekend of "haunted camp" she decided to stay behind. With all five of them sharing a three bedroom house she was, at least at first, happy to have them out of the house.

After a few hours, and as the sun began to set, she realized she had never been alone in this house for more than a few hours. She hadn't even slept alone; she shared a room with Lissa. While in the shower that first night a thump echoed through the empty rooms. Grabbing the plunger to use as some sort of weapon against whatever made the noise she stepped slowly around the corner to see her roommate's cat standing over a knocked down bowl of leftovers.

Chuckling at her own paranoia she went back to her shower. Returning to the bathroom she was shocked to find that the shower was off, but she shrugged it off as a subconscious move. Curling up on the couch with her would-be-attacker/cat she flipped listlessly through the channels, unsuccessfully trying to find anything new or non-reality: Even the Halloween shows were reruns. As the night crawled on a sense of being watched started to grow stronger and stronger, Jennah nervously started checking the windows and locks every few minutes. For the rest of the night she went on, unsleeping and curled under the covers jumping at every creak. On the fourth night of paranoia, brought on by a barrage of constant noises, Jennah was relieved to know that this was her last night alone. It was Halloween and her friends would be back in the morning.

Around midnight the water in the kitchen turned on and her bed shook under her. She braved to put her feet on the floor before running to the living room where she turned on every light. Retrieving a knife from the kitchen as she turned the water faucet off Jennah scanned the room. She knew someone had been watching her, they knew this was her last night alone and now they were messing with her. The cabinets began to slam open and closed repeatedly while water ran from every faucet in the house. The locked windows flew open and shut as the door struggled to open against the chair placed across it.

Somehow Jennah was able to fall asleep amongst the chaos. After closing her eyes for what seemed like only moments she felt a tug at her blanket. Screaming Jennah lunged at the intruder with the knife, but tangled in the blankets, fell on it herself. Lissa screamed for help but by the time the ambulance came it was too late. After seeing the house, it was obvious to everyone that Jennah had a psychotic break. With no one around to help her she had destroyed the apartment and then herself.

Rebecca Carter *is an upcoming horror and suspense author newly focused on the human monster. Her first self published release 'Moonlit Daydreams is currently available in print and eBook format. For more information on Rebecca Carter visit rebeccacarterbooks.com*

Candy Ban
By Maurice Vaughan

In a few hours, dawn will sweep this moderate-sized Kansas neighborhood. The demonic decorations and eerie atmosphere signal that it's Halloween. Only a handful of parents and their young children are out trick 'r treating.

A 9-year-old trick 'r treater dressed as a ninja shuffles down the sidewalk with a stuffed bag of candy mounted over his shoulder. He stops at a plain two-story home and stares at the front door. He sits the bag down and rafts through it. He emerges with a few miniature candy bars; the good kind. He flops down on the curve and devours the sweet treats while occasionally peeking over his shoulder at the home.

Orange mist mangled with black smoke drifts to the street and screens the sidewalks. The treater is too busy munching on his sweet rewards to notice. A wind storm forms above the homes, kicking over trash cans and jack-o-lanterns and beating against the parked vehicles. Rain showers down in the form of candy. The treater notices the candy piling up around him. Unsure of the reason behind the falling treats, he stuffs some into his already full bag.

The storm and raining candy stop. Silence takes their place. The shadow of an obese candy creature appears over the treater. The treater looks up, face plastered with chocolate, peanuts and caramel. The creature's body looks like a Halloween costume. It's made of sticky caramel with candy pieces and dead insects trapped inside it. His head and skin resemble rotten candy corn. The fat around his neck causes him to breathe loudly. At the end of his fat fingers are razor hooks. With his left hand he mounts a behemoth bag of candy on his shoulder.

"Hi. Cool candy costume. It looks sticky," the treater says, smiling and showing the candy residue on his choppers.

The creature doesn't reply.

"What's your name?" the treater asks.

"Candy Ban," the ugly monster mumbles, revealing the chocolate flavored drool dripping from his dagger teeth.

The treater becomes scared and grips his bag of candy in an attempt to protect it from the possible candy snatcher. He looks back at the home as if trying to spot help. With no help present, he faces the creature and swallows the candy reserve sitting in his mouth.

"Do you want a piece of candy?" the treater asks, more of a plea to be spared than to be friendly.

"You should never eat your candy before you get home," Candy Ban utters.

"This is my home. Behind me," the treater replies.

Candy Ban's breathing grows louder as if excited by the treater's answer.

The treater reaches in his bag and brings out a peanut butter Halloween taffy. He holds it out to Candy Ban.

"It's good candy," the treater announces.

Candy Ban slaps the treater's hand, knocking the taffy away. The treater curls his abused hand to his chest.

"That hurt!" he wails, eyes filling with tears. Blood gushes from the deep gashes on his hand.

"I'm telling my dad on you!" he protests, getting up and heading toward the home. Before he takes another step, he's face first on the ground. Candy Ban latches onto the treater's kicking limbs. The treater claws at the dirt and grabs for help that's not there. Candy Ban releases the horrendous moan of an undead savage. The treater kicks free. He hops to his feet and darts for the porch.

Atop the porch, he swings around in his ninja stance and lets out a high-pitched ninja squall. He looks at the front door. No one comes to it. He sees sticky caramel dripping off his pants where Candy Ban grabbed. He spots his bag of candy lumped on the curve.

He swallows the fear hanging stiff in his throat and ninja steps down the porch. His shaking legs make it hard for him to keep his balance.

He scats to the curve and snatches up his candy. He turns to run back, but Candy Ban places his candy bag over him.

The treater collapses to the ground, entrapped inside the bag. Candy Ban slings it over his shoulder and wobbles away. The treater scratches at the bag to carve through. The crackling of bones inside the bag mashes with his vain screams for help.

Maurice Vaughan *is an experienced fiction screenwriter, aspiring video game writer and a hobbyist short story writer. The key genres he writes within are Sci-Fi, Fantasy, Adventure, Action, Horror, Thriller and Animation. He plans to continue writing anthology stories and have them published in many more amazing anthology books.*

A Night's Work
By Diandra Linnemann

Unloading the barrels was the hardest part. In the dark, Steve almost fell over a dead branch the size of a small alligator. He held his breath and cursed. If everything went down smoothly, there was good money in it for them. Easy money.

He glanced back over his shoulder at Ralph. "Come on, sicko, hurry up!"

"Don't rush me, man," Ralph replied under his breath. He was struggling to open the dented back of the truck. Flaky paint sailed to the ground. He wiped sweat from his brow and, in the process, left a dark smear on his oily skin. Despite the cold October air, the neatly ironed METALLICA T-shirt was glued to his massive chest.

Steve grinned. No use telling Mrs. Whitly that ironing was not heavy metal.

"Let's find a place first, before we drag that shit out of the car!"

Ralph paused his struggle with the truck. "You sure this is the right location? How we gonna get this stuff packed away?"

"With the barrow, of course! Stupid."

Ralph smirked. "Man, you show me how to drag the barrels through the wilderness on a barrow. You Superman, right?"

"Got any better ideas?" Steve slapped his arm in an attempt to draw first blood in tonight's battle between man and mosquito. He missed. "Maybe we should stack that shit in your mother's garage?"

"No way, man!"

"Okay then, let's roll."

As quiet as possible, the men trudged through the dead bushes in their Doc Martens.

Ralph was surely right about the difficulties concerning transportation – but Steve would rather be dipped in honey and tied to a tree in bear country, naked, than admitting to that. They'd have to carry the barrels. But apart from that, the place was perfect. There were no houses, no recreational activities going on, and dense vegetation and headlands on either side protected them from being seen from further away. They looked around a bit, decided to cover everything with dry branches to delay detection, and hiked back up to the truck.

"By the way, man, what's inside them?" Ralph slapped himself in the face. "Damn mosquitoes!"

Steve shrugged. "Don't know, something chemical."

Ralph rolled his eyes. "Didn't you pay attention in high school? *Everything's* chemical!"

"So what? Joshua said, get rid of it, and not to get anything on ourselves." Steve chuckled. "He said it'd burn holes right through us."

"You think he's serious?"

"No way, man! Believe me, that stuff's harmless. He just don't want to pay for disposal. You know Josh."

They started unloading. None of them noticed the sulfur eyes watching them.

The barrels were heavier than they looked, and the men stumbled under their sloshing, gargling load. Soon they decided they needed a break. Both grabbed a beer from the passenger foot space.

"Why you always buying this piss?" Ralph glared at the label.

"German beer is the best."

"Bitter piss, that's what it is!"

Steve grabbed the bottle from his friend's hand. "No one forcing you to drink it. More for me!" He threw his head back and emptied the first bottle.

"Hey, give it back!" Ralph snatched the second bottle from Steve's hand. "You gonna get drunk while I do all the work?" His full-moon-shaped face was pink and sweaty. He was feeling a little bit dizzy and wondered if there might be weird fumes.

They returned to work. Only five more barrels. Afterwards, they'd head back to town, to the annual Halloween bar brawl, with steaks and fries and whisky, and a hug – or more – from Patty the waitress. Everybody knew Patty was a friendly girl.

Their repeated trips had formed a broad path clearly visible from the street, even in the dark. All they could hope for was that no one would use this street anytime soon, and that if somebody did, no one would remember having seen them around here. Of course, since it was Halloween... they might just as well be the only humans on a desert planet.

The hiss sounded so much like part of the nightly lake concert that at first the men didn't register the words. But when the beast put its scaled head next to Ralph's, they froze. "Ssstopp!"

Steve felt as if he had been catapulted back into his high school drug experiments. His eyes widened. He looked straight past Ralph, turned to stone by the sight. "Whatever you do, sicko, don't turn around."

Of course Ralph turned around.

He shrieked like a little girl and let go of his end of the barrel. Steve was yanked forward with mechanical force, and with a clang and a gurgle, the barrel rolled down the slope. It crashed into a tree and stopped about twenty feet away from them. The gurgling sound continued for a few seconds.

"Don't move!" The beast's voice was deep and rumbling and wrapped itself around the hard sounds as if it would swallow them together with glass shards.

"We're not moving!" Steve suggested with a thin whine. This was unlike everything he had ever imagined. And Ralph could obviously see it, too. That could only mean one thing – mass hallucination! Poisonous fumes! He held his breath to avoid further contamination, and almost instantly started feeling dizzy.

The beast advanced, crossing the line between the men, watching them carefully. Its greenish humanoid body was almost invisible between the darkness and the dry leaves.

Steve tried to swallow, but the lump in his throat would not budge. That creature must be close to seven feet tall! The sulfur gaze made him feel small and insignificant. His eyes flickered to Ralph, he saw a dark stain on his friend's pants. Well, he surely wasn't the only one to be afraid.

After sniffing the fallen barrel for a few moments, thoroughly, crouching on the ground on all fours, the creature turned around and hissed. A forked tongue protruded from thin lips, glistening grayish-blue in the truck's headlights. "What issss thisss?"

"Nothing?" Ralph suggested.

"And what are you doing with it?"

Ralph's face lost its healthy color as the strange creature approached him. He looked at Steve, urging him to help out somehow, to come up with a brilliant plan that would save their asses. "Uhm, we were... stashing them away in a safe place."

"And... where would that sssafe plasssse be?"

"Don't ask me! It was his idea!" Ralph turned around and tried to run.

That coward!

Steve watched and couldn't exactly make out if he wanted to smirk or cry when that – thing launched itself at his friend and swept him off his feet with a growl. "I sssaid, don't move!" Talons ripped through the soft meat on Ralph's arm, and the man screamed with pain as he was dragged to his feet and past Steve. His free arm shot out in search of help and grabbed his friend.

"Let go!" Steve struggled, but the beast turned around and grabbed him as well. Everything happened in a blur, and then he felt himself airborne for a second, followed by hard contact with something metallic. He struggled to get to his feet. The air from the lake smelled like rain, and the nights' sounds had ceased. Only the softest lapping of tiny waves over pebbles let him know that the fall had not burst his eardrums. He marveled at the strange quality of things.

"You claim thisss isss harmlessssss?" The creature's glance darted back and forth between them.

"Well, yes, of course!" Steve tried to appear trustworthy. He felt something warm and sticky running down his back. He staggered and fell back against a barrel.

"Then drink." The creature's talons sliced the lid of one of the barrels. A brain-piercing stench rose from the gashes. The mosquitoes took flight immediately.

"You must be mad!" Steve exclaimed. "I..." His sentence stopped as the beast reached out to him, lifted him off the ground and almost casually ripped out his trachea. Eyes bulging, he fell back to his knees. He realized that the whizzing sound was made by his own body fighting for survival, and then the world turned black.

Ralph soiled his pants, the second time in less than ten minutes. Strange enough, he didn't feel ashamed. He would have walked all the way into town in his messed-up pants, if only that thing would let him live.

The creature turned around to him and, maybe, smiled. It was hard to tell with all the scales. "I ssssaid, drink!"

Ralph hesitated, and the black talon dug further into his arm. For one moment the pain was excruciating, and then the sensation disappeared. Surely that was not a good sign. He took a step forward, bent over the barrel. The smell made him nauseous. He lowered his face to the sickening liquid and felt his eyes starting to water. His lips touched the gleaming surface.

The pain took a moment to register with his brain, then Ralph started to scream. He didn't scream for very long.

Diandra Linnemann*, born 1982, is a translator and writer and shares a flat with her two weird cats, a boyfriend and about a dozen dying plants. If she isn't writing, she likes to run, cook and go out for sushi with friends. She has published German and English stories in several anthologies and magazines and can be found and read online at* http://www.shortstoriesandmadrants.blogspot.com*.*

Zombies Don't Trick or Treat
By Rusty Fischer

The zombies were out
For a fun, festive night;
They were goblins and ghouls
And witches in sight.

Over there was a demon
His legs warm as toast;
Down that street's a pumpkin
Down that one's a ghost.

No, it wasn't Armageddon
Or a monster's pot luck;
It was the one mortal night
That didn't quite... *suck*!

That's right, little ghosties
It was... *Halloween*;
The creepiest, crawliest
Living dead scene!

Poor Chester was frightened
He was new to this town;
And ever since dying
Poor Chester'd been down.

He wasn't quite used
To being undead;
If he had *his* way
He'd be living... instead.

His friends *liked* being zombies
They found it quite cool;
But all Chester felt
Was like one giant fool!

He hated his hairdo
He hated his skin;
He hated the fact
That he could no longer grin.

His legs they were stiff
His arms were quite chilly;
And stumbling around
Just made Chester feel... silly.

Tonight might be different
Poor Chester agreed;
As he watched other kids
Look as foolish as he.

For each one looked goofy
For each one looked grim;
For each one looked not
Quite much better than... him!

"But where are they going?"
He asked of a bud;
Who looked at him like
He had the IQ of a spud.

"They're all trick-or-treating,"
Was the answer he gave;
"Or have you forgotten,
Since you rose from the grave?"

"I seem to recall,"
Little Chester did say;
"Of begging for candy
On Halloween day."

"Let's give it a try,"
His buddy made it sound like a
synch;
"Chocolate's not as good as brains
But it'll do in a pinch."
Chester shrugged
And followed his friend;
As they shuffled and groaned
Up the long driveway's end.

The lawn was festooned
With orange and black;
The setting quite ripe
For a zombie attack!

The young man who stood
At his cozy front door;
Thought the zombies on his
porch
Wore costumes; nothing more.

He smiled,
They shuffled;
He sniffed

And he snuffled.

"I quite love your costumes,"
He said with a smile.
"But your breath I smelled com-
ing
For more than a mile!"

When the man tried to offer
A bowl full of candy;
All Chester could smell
Was his brain oh-so-dandy.

He reached for the bowl
But dropped it instead;
And as the man bent to catch it
Clamped onto his head.

"But why?" asked the man
Squealing in pain;
"Why bother with candy,"
Chester said
"When my **treat** is… your
brain!"

Rusty Fischer *is the author of several YA supernatural novels, including* Zombies Don't Cry, Ushers, Inc., Vamplayers, I Heart Zombie *and* Panty Raid @ Zombie High. *Visit his blog,* www.zombiesdontblog.blogspot.com, *for news, reviews, cover leaks, writing and publishing advice, book excerpts and more!*

Driving Alone
By Jimalyn Lawless

Billowing clouds of dust followed as the car travelled along the road. On either side of the road, peeling bark hung from gum trees in shapes resembling dangling bodies. The setting sun flashed on the windscreen temporarily blinding the driver. Bruce glanced at the scrap of paper that held the directions he must follow. A shiver ran through his body, and he reached for his jacket laying on the passenger seat. Was it the weather making the hairs on his arm stand on end, or what he was about to do? Either way he would be glad when this was over.

He turned off the road at the sight of the gate with the dried skull, horns protruding and a dead snake threaded through one eye. As he stepped out, he felt the warmth fade from the evening, and another shiver ran through his body. The long road to the house gleamed golden in the setting sun. Driving toward the house, he could hear the warning barks of dogs and hoped they were chained up. His wounds had only just healed from the last encountered. He had hardly left the seat of the car when the Rottweiler came charging around the corner, froth dripping from its huge jaws, and teeth gleaming as it snarled, it grabbed hold of Bruce's leg and ripped. Bruce tried to pull away as pain shot through his leg. Eventually he managed to fight the beast off and climb into the car slamming the door. He didn't relish the idea of fighting off another attack.

As he approached the house, he saw two men in blue bib and brace overalls towering over an older woman he guessed to be about seventy. Dirt stained her clothes, and grim encrusted her fingernails. He walked to the back of the station wagon to get the equipment he needed, then headed toward the house noticing as he did that the woman's eyes were red from crying, the men too mopped up tears with dirt and blood stained handkerchiefs. The woman led the way inside.

"Wipe your feet," she snapped as she went through the kitchen, down the hall and into the bedroom. Bed springs sagged under the weight of the body. Blood crusted his forehead and smeared his overalls.

"Poppa," Bruce heard one of the boys blurt out through his tears, and turned to see the two men standing behind him.

As Bruce prepared the stretcher, he wondered if it would hold the body. One of the boys helped Bruce manoeuvre the body onto the stretcher. He could hear the creaks as he wheeled it to the car. This brought on more tears from the woman and sniffs from the men who were now standing with their arms draped around their mother's shoulders. Bruce offered his condolences before starting on the journey back to town. He was glad to be leaving, he hadn't felt at ease since he'd arrived, something was strange about that place. The front of the van was slightly higher with the weight in the back. Once on the road back to town, Bruce turned on the headlights, it was getting very dark and there was that chill in the air again. He felt bumps in the road he hadn't felt before. He also imagined he heard noises coming from the back, but wasn't going to turn around to have a look.

Don't be silly, he thought, this man is dead and dead men don't talk. As he approached the town, the car went over a bump left from recent road works. Bruce heard a loud burp that seemed to go forever. Turning, he saw the corpse sitting bolt up right, his eyes fixed on Bruce. He stopped the car, opened the door and ran like hell.

And as he ran he heard a scream coming from the car.

"WHERE THE BLOODY HELL AM I?"

Jimalyn Lawless has been interested in poetry and writing short stories for about 15 years, but any form of visual art interest her. She has one poem published in a magazine in Australia called Positive Words.

The Spell
By Lyle Perez-Tinics

"What do you mean by not invited?" Joey asked, holding the house phone between his ear and shoulder. He continued to wrap gauze around his body.

Joey decided to go all out with his Halloween costume, more so than previous years. One Halloween, Joey wanted to be Frankenstein's monster, but all of the store costumes were cheaply made. The young boy decided to paint himself green from head to toe and even rubbed dead, decaying animals on his body to give him that real death smell. That's how dedicated he was.

This year, Joey was going to go as a mummy. He wanted that sense of realism in his costume so he had been wrapping his nude body with medical gauze. He was going to have the best costume at the Halloween party. At least he thought.

"Listen Joey," the person on the phone began, "Suzy shouldn't have invited you today at school. I told her not too. You won't have any fun here."

"Fine!" Joey spat, dropping the roll of gauze. "I didn't even want to go to your stupid party. In fact, I have other things to do, more adult things than going to some stupid thirteen-year-old girl's party." Joey hung up the phone.

He felt emptiness in his belly. His plans for the night were completely ruined. The truth was he had nothing else to do. He even told his mother he was invited to a Halloween party and that he wasn't going to go trick-or-treating this year.

He began to unwrap himself and put on his pajamas. If he really wanted to, he could have finished putting on his mummy costume and ran after his mom and little brother. They were out in the neighborhood trick-or-treating, but he was told to stay home and hand out candy 'til they came back.

Walking downstairs to the living area, Joey grabbed a book off one of the shelves, sat down and began reading. A few minutes later, the doorbell rang.

"Trick-or-treat," the kids cheered as he opened the door.

"Well, well... trick-or-treaters. Here's one for you and you," he paused to look at the third kid. "Nothing for you. Your costume looks like crap." He slammed the door in their faces.

His invitation being revoked left its toll on Joey. All he wanted now was for his mom and brother to come home so he could lock himself in his room.

He had just sat back down with his book when the doorbell rang again.

Joey grabbed the bowl of candy and yanked open the door. Standing before him were four tall guys. He estimated them to be at least twice his age.

"Can I help you guys?" he asked.

"Trick-or-treat," the man in the middle said, holding out his bag for a treat. He was wearing a bleach white shirt, while everyone else was in black.

Joey looked at him with a questionable expression.

"Aren't you guys too old to be trick-or-treating?"

"No," the same guy answered.

"Well you guys don't even have costumes, so move on," Joey barked and shoved the door, but it didn't shut. One of them put his leg in-between the doorway causing the door to swing back.

"You're going to give us candy," the guy in white said.

"I'm not doing anything."

All four of them walked into the house. One of them yanked the bowl of candy out of Joey's hands while another one swung his arms behind him, holding Joey in place.

"Next time, just give us the candy." The man in white closed his fist and punched Joey in the gut. Carbon dioxide rushed out of him like a gust of wind. The guy hit him three more times before letting go. Joey fell limp to the ground, gasping for air like a fish with no water. They laughed and walked out the door, closing it behind them.

Joey's eyes filled with tears. He was in pain, he was sad and he was angry. Joey clawed himself to the living area and reached the book he was reading. He sat down and stared at the title, *Ancient Witchcraft of Revenge*. Finding the correct page, Joey began chanting.

"Mistress of the dark, please hear my cries. Please feel my pain, help me fight the ones who caused, as for their life I will drain. With the heat from the sun, their candy will run, their mouths will close, and then they are done."

***

The four men who stole Joey's candy sat around a square dining room table as they did every year. Stealing candy on Halloween night was nothing new to them. All of them got a laugh out of doing this.

They dumped the stolen treats on the table.

"Did you see how scared that kid was?"

"I think he wet his pants."

The laughter grew heavier.

"Let's dig in!"

They searched the candy for their most desired sweet. When they all found the piece they wanted to start with, they peeled away the wrapper and shoved the candy into their mouths.

"So freaking good."

They began to search for their second piece when suddenly, all of their mouths began to burn. They tried to spit out the candy, but their mouths wouldn't open. The piece of candy felt like it was a hot coal. They tried to scream but couldn't. Their tongue sizzled from the heat; their taste buds were completely burned off. Steam smoked out of their noses. They stood from their chairs and tried to pry their mouths open. There was nothing they could do. One by one, they swallowed the coal like candy.

Lyle Perez-Tinics is the owner of Rainstorm Press. He is also a zombie book reviewer, his reviews can be found at www.UndeadintheHead.com. Lyle is the author of many short stories. His work can be found on Amazon.
Find him on Facebook www.Facebook.com/UndeadinthHead
Find him on Twitter www.Twitter.com/LylePerez
Email him at Lyle@RainstomePress.com

Lights Out
By Kevin Walsh

Whenever the family went camping, their favorite game to play was Yahtzee, mainly due to the fact that it was more of a game of chance than anything else. Michael—Timmy and Katie's father—sat adjacent to Katie, meanwhile their mother, Vanessa, was in the trailer making a midnight snack.

Their trailer was parked at one of the campsites in the Red Sault's islands. Uncle Chris and Uncle George played the game as well, enjoying a few drinks and their off-color cajolery made Vanessa think twice about an encore invitation.

The campfire blazed a few yards away, supplying the small campsite with a meager brilliance. Michael looked at his bickering children, than back to the dense woods. Thick foliage blocked their view of other nearby campsites, with small copses of trees and brushes serving as adequate obstructions. They resumed the game and eventually Tommy won, making for his fifth consecutive victory. Uncle Chris and George sighed in disbelief, but Michael could only grin, knowing very well that his son could master any game he played. Psychologists have told Michael that Tommy was incredibly smart. This idea was supported by Tommy's superior grade average, and he eventually skipped two grades. Michael did everything in his power to nurture his son's mind, even if that meant getting his ass kicked, ten times out of ten in chess. The father's pride doubled as he learned that his daughter was showing some of the same mental equivalency as her brother.

Tommy left the table and walked toward the fire, a somber wind rushed up his back as he looked skyward. Something in the sky intrigued him. Michael looked up and saw a clear sky, canopied with stars and not a single cloud was present in the night's canvas. He was about to say something to him, but his attention was drawn to Uncle George, who fiddled with the radio.

It kept spewing static, the faint murmurs of a song was distorted through the haze.

"Goddamn thing! That was my favorite fu-"

"Language!" Vanessa hollered from inside the trailer, cutting off

Uncle George before he could let loose a volley of invectives in front of her children.

He apologized. "Sorry...it was as clear as a bell a moment ago, but now it's all snow."

"Well maybe it would work if you stopped hitting it," Michael chortled as Uncle George shot him a shit-eating grin.

"But that's so weird...maybe AM will be different."

Uncle George's fingers fiddled with the dial and he let go as he found a clear signal.

"SHHHHHHHHH...They're here! They're really here! SHHHH- the National Guard has arrived. Tanks and soldiers are in the street, canvassing fo- SHHHHHH." The static made the radio host's voice almost unintelligible.

"What the hell?" Uncle George muttered before being hushed by Michael and Chris.

"SHHH- we can't get a clear view of them...we can't see them, there's gunfire. SHHHH. Light is coming from the alleyway, man, it's bright. *SLAM* SHHHH, They're in the radio station! SHHHH."

Dead air.

"Get it back, bro," Chris demanded as he fumbled with the dial once more.

"WAHHHHN!" a high pitched, abnormal wail pierced through the speaker.

"Balishatistala! Kahliszeligar, *tick tick* Zebaniskaliquera, *tick tick* WAHHHHHN"

Everybody looked at the radio with astonishment. Vanessa walked out of the trailer, clearly trouble by the radio. She turned it off. "Enough of that, we must have picked up a foreign signal or somethin'...anywho! Anybody want to come inside for a snack then we will roast some marshmallows, how does that sound?"

"I'm in," George and Chris said in tandem and they went in the trailer.

"Katie, want to come in?" Vanessa asked with a smile.

"No, it's okay, I want to stay out here with daddy."

Vanessa smile was a lie, she was a little perturbed by the radio and something didn't feel right to her. She went back inside, closing the door behind her.

Tommy continued looking into the sky, as if he were trying to identify constellations. Michael couldn't help but ponder, *What is he looking at? What's up th-* His train of thought was derailed by yells coming from all over the campground; the camper's distressed cries piqued Michael's curiosity.

"What the hell is that about?" Vanessa yelled to Michael, she heard the same screams as he did.

The shouts were amplified, Michael hearkened to the voices, but he couldn't determine what was being said. A loud ringing sound pulsed through the air, and the lantern they used for their games flickered. The lamp went dead in the same instant as the light from within the trailer, making the campfire the only source of light in the campground. Its orange brilliance continued to dance, throwing shadows onto everything, each one given its own human-esque characteristics. It was like they were surrounded.

He heard commotion from inside the trailer, Vanessa's voice sounded terrified, but Michael's attention was drawn to his children.

"Timmy, please come over here," said Michael, his voice cracked.

Timmy continued looking skyward, like a statue.

Michael was going to ask again but his attention was seized by a noise.

"SHHHH- Catystabhecala! Spykelpzerty, WAAAAAHN!" blared from the radio, which had turned on by itself.

The radio shut off and a blinding light illuminated the campsite from above, as if on cue. It covered everything in a white pitch, and Timmy was looking straight at it.

Michael's thoughts rushed, *What the hell is that noise? The light...*

The trailer started glowing, light spewed from each of the windows and he thought he heard something that resembled a malfunctioning microwave, and the trailer shook.

Run! Get the kids out of here, now! Was the only thought in his mind, instinctive and demanding. He figured his wife would be fine from whatever it was, but he needed to protect his children.

Run now or it will be too late..what's happening?...are they visitors?...aliens?

Michael picked up his daughter and did the same to Tommy after running over. He hesitated before running to their car, which ran parallel with the road. There was a beam of light slowly creeping along the gravel, going toward the car. Driving wasn't an option. *They* were coming, whoever *they* were

"Hold on," he said to his children—who were hoisted over each shoulder--as he ran to the tree line.

Branches swatted his face and pinpricks of thorns hacked at his shins, tearing his clothes and flesh, but this didn't deter Michael. He needed to run and bring his kids to safety. The woods were consumed in an inky, unforgiving darkness. More shouts filled the air, they sounded closer than before, but Michael's attention was brought to a glow from the corner of his eyes, behind him.

They are coming for me!

Beams of light spilled through some of the trees and the voices grew in faculty. The voices were more aggressive than before, but he still couldn't determine what was being said.

They drew closer.

Several beams of light poked through the trees, coming from nearly every direction, Michael tried to run in the opposite direction, but he soon found himself surrounded. The combined weight of his children on his shoulder was burdensome and he finally put them down on their feet, breathing heavily as he looked around. The lights were approaching from all over.

"Freeze, don't move!" A voice shouted and a beam of light fell upon Michael's face.

Eight more beams fell on him. As he squinted, he saw that each of these men adorned black suits, sunglasses and some of them carried automatic firearms. The light from above illuminated the area around him and he realized that it was a search helicopter.

They looked human.

Michael's eyes widened as he looked at his kids. Timmy and Katie's eyes were bulbous, veins as thick as cables pulsated beneath their pallid skin, which seemed to glow. Coal black eyes stared back at him, without a sign of recognition. Their mouths moved silently, speaking in a tongue nobody can hear as their bodies slightly twitched.

They were searching for my kids...they disguised themselves as my children...their intelligence...Timmy's fascination with the sky...no, it can't be.

He heard one final shout before he was struck on the back of the head. Everything went dark as he collapsed and fell unconscious.

Kevin Walsh *is an aspiring horror novelist who has published (or about to publish) short stories in various anthologies by Rainstorm Press, Pill Hill Press, Coscom Entertainment, Library of the Living Dead and Knight-Watch Press. He invites people to check out his free online zombie novel at http://genocidexzombienovel.blogspot.com/*

Lorelie
By J. Rodimus Fowler

October 17th

*"Lorelie is coming for you.
Lorelie is coming for you.
There's nothing you can do,
Lorelie is coming for you."*

The other kids on the playground were chanting that horrible song as Ricky and Steve chased Josh to the top of the sliding board. Steve waited for Josh at the bottom of the slide while Ricky climbed up the ladder behind him. He was caught like a moth in a spider's web. The rest of their class gathered all around the slide with their snickering and their chanting. *"Lorelie Lorelie!"* Then one of them blurted out, "Look at that, the scaredy cat wet himself. He peed his pants!"

Ricky hopped backwards from the ladder and fell down to his knees with laughter. Steve quickly started laughing as well and one by one, all the other children began to giggle. Tears formed in Josh's eyes and his face turned red with embarrassment. He jumped down the slide on his knees and ran off to the bathroom as soon as he reached the bottom. No one tried to chase him, not even the two bullies.

Josh ran into the farthest stall away from the entrance to the bathroom and sat on the toilet. He was barely crying now, but his face was still red. He wiped the tears from his eyes on to the sleeves of his shirt, took a handful of toilet paper and was about to blow his nose when all of a sudden he heard a girls' voice, though he couldn't make out what she said. One of the two fluorescent lights on the ceiling began to hum loudly and blinked off and on. After a few hypnotic flashes it went out completely. The stall that josh was hiding in grew very dim.

Josh stood and reached for the lock on the stall door. Before his hand ever touched the handle, the remaining light went out. He was quickly frozen with fear. The bathroom door opened and shut followed by the sound of footsteps across the tile floor. Josh spoke up,

"Hey the lights went out. Can you cut them on?" A still silence floated in the air.

"Hello is anybody out there? Mrs. Hamilton is that you?"

Josh thought that it might be her checking on him since he ran off to the bathroom without asking for permission, and the fact that he had heard a girls voice just before. He thought it may have been her talking in the hallway.

Once again no one answered him. Josh backed away from the door slowly until he felt the rim of the toilet touch the back of his leg, which made him jump with fright. Suddenly, the sink cut on and the sounds of running water filled the bathroom.

"Mrs. Hamilton! Mrs. Hamilton is that you?"

After a minute of silence that felt more like an eternity, Josh's mind began to fill with the sounds of the children's earlier chanting. *'Lorelie is coming for you!'*

The story of Lorelie played through his head like a movie. She was a little girl that went to the same school years earlier. She had left school with a sickness, but was supposed to have been well when she returned a few months later. She came back sickly looking with no hair, so none of the other kids at school would play with her, not even her friends from before she was ill. She spent the last days of her life alone, wanting a friend more than anything in the whole world. She never got one. She died unexpectedly a couple of weeks later in school, right in the middle of class. The story says that she still haunts the school looking for a friend, for someone to play with.

A little girl began to giggle quietly from outside the stall. Josh's knuckles turned white with fear, his breath began to come in short spurts and his pulse was racing. Someone pounded on the stall door almost hard enough to break the little metal latch. They pounded on the door three more times with equal force. Josh stood up on the bowl and pressed his back against the wall behind him. Every muscle in his body was trembling and he wet himself again. He started sobbing and drooling as he pleaded, "Leave me alone. Go away, please go away. Please, please, please."

The sound of a girl giggling came from right beside him. He looked over to his left and there was a little girls head peeking up at him from above the stall next door. The girl was ghostly pale and her flesh resembled the side of the moon through a telescope. There were dark splotches and veins showing through her translucent flesh. Her eyes scared Josh the most, they were two black holes that emptied into a bleak hollow nothingness. Her nose consisted of two small slits just above her mouth. Just as Josh was about to look away, her frail little lips formed into a smile, further adding to the horror of her appearance. She whispered, "Peek-a-boo."

Josh jumped down to the floor and backed as far away as the other wall would let him. The little girl's face disappeared into the other stall and she started giggling again outside of the door. Josh screamed aloud, "Mrs. Hamilton! Mrs. Hamilton!"

The bathroom door opened up and the footsteps entered the room. There was a clicking sound and the lights blinked twice and came back on. Mrs. Hamilton's voice spoke up, "Josh are you OK? Josh... are you in here?"

Josh was relieved to say the least, with tears still in his eyes, he opened the stall door and ran out to greet his teacher. When he stepped out past the stalls, the room was empty. Mrs. Hamilton wasn't there, no one was there. The sink beside him turned on by itself and a giggling rang out through the bathroom. Josh turned around and the little girl, with her sad empty eyes, was standing right behind him. The lights went out.

After finding out about what happened to Josh on the playground, Mrs. Hamilton went to see if he was alright. When she went inside the bathroom it was completely empty. After sealing off the school and calling in every emergency officer in town, they couldn't find Josh. The search went on all through the night and several days later, but the results were the same. Josh was never found.

October 31st - Halloween Night

The school's Halloween party was almost over when Ricky saw scrawny little Thomas walk through the double doors and out into the hallway. It was against school rules to leave the gymnasium during the party, so he grabbed Steve and followed behind Thomas to see what he was doing or to maybe instill some fear in the puny little boy. They made sure no teachers or chaperones saw them on their way out.

Ricky and Steve walked behind Thomas, who was acting very strange. He was dressed up as a mummy for the party and acted the part; he was walking very rigid and stiff. Ricky said, "Hey man, knock it off. We know you saw us."

Thomas never looked back, he just moved up the hallway slowly into the darkness, only the red exit signs were illuminating the hallway this far away from the party.

Steve hollered out, "Cut it out Thomas!"

The mummy stopped walking and stood still with his back to the bullies. A girl's laughter echoed through the hallway behind the boys. When they turned to see, a boy's laughter started up from Thomas' direction, but when they looked back Thomas had vanished. The hallway was clear as far as the eye could see, which wasn't possible.

Steve pushed past Ricky almost knocking him down, and began to run for the gymnasium doors. Ricky followed suit, but stopped running as soon as he saw the little girl and boy standing at the other end of the hall where they were headed. Ricky saw the black of their eyes and the boy's face. The little girl and boy held hands and began to skip up the hallway toward Steve and Ricky, they were still giggling. Ricky peed in his pants, fell to the floor and fainted right that second.

Ricky woke up to someone caressing his arm and his mother's voice asking if he was alright. He rubbed his weary eyes and looked up to ask, *what happened to Steve*. As soon as his eyes adjusted he realized he was still on the floor in the dark school hallway and his mother was nowhere to be found. A pale little girl with thin skin and black holes for eyes was in her place and Josh, with black eyes as well, was standing beside her holding Steve's severed head in his hand like a jack o' lantern. He looked down and said, "Wanna play?"

Jason Rodimus Fowler was born in 1976 and hails from Raleigh, North Carolina, where he began a life-long passion for anything horror related. When he was twelve years old or so his mother handed him a copy of Clive Barker's The Damnation Game, and it changed his life forever. J. Rodimus began to write short horror fiction with a flair for dark comedy. His twisted tales of fear and retribution range from battling hordes of the undead, to true love among demon fodder.

Wretched
By R. M. Cochran

They only appear at night when the world is calm and everything has gone quiet. From the corner of your eye, they bounce between reality and dream. It flashes so quick that you're not sure if you actually saw anything at all. From the edge of the closet or around the nightstand they appear for a moment to gaze at you through vicious eyes of red, watching your heart skip a beat and they are gone again. Just long enough to steal your breath away.

You saw them while you were sitting in your chair, getting ready for bed. From your peripheral vision, it came like a cloak of shadow and smiled. But as you looked toward the kitchen, it was gone. Shaken, you stared toward the apparition, hoping to catch another glimpse. It was nowhere to be found. It was as if it had never existed at all.

A few months later, after having moved your chair away from the corner of the living room, your wife saw the twisted nothingness. She jerked with a start and shook her head, pretending she didn't see anything at all.

"What's the matter?" you ask.

"I thought I saw something in the kitchen. But when I looked, it was gone."

You are not sure if you should tell her that you have seen it too. There is a knock in your chest as your heart skips a beat. Suddenly, your mouth is dry and you have trouble trying to speak.

"Was it thin with a long neck and boney limbs?" you ask, mustering the courage.

"Yes, exactly, how did you know?" she is taken aback.

"I've seen it too."

With a numbness that tingles along your spine, you recount what you have seen. The memories are like dreams peeled away from nothingness and fantasy. The shadow, at first didn't have any eyes, nor a mouth. It was nothing but a smoky blob of darkness in an already blackened room. It leaned around the corner of the refrigerator and vanished as soon as you realized it was there.

But your wife, she was able to catch more than a glimpse. Maybe it was that extra tenth of a second, but she saw its eyes flash red and a tangled mess of mouth open wide before it smiled and receded back into nothingness.

You left the light on in the bathroom from that time forward, afraid of what it might do if it had a chance to move freely. Time passed, just enough for you to get comfortable again. Just long enough for it to change its ways. Just long enough for you to forget what you had seen.

The mind is a fickle thing and you forgot to turn on the light one night. In a state of terror, you saw it again. It leered at you for longer than it ever had before. It held up a single digit as its face transformed into hideousness and wretched decay. It mocked your fear. It gasped in laughter and vanished. You couldn't tell your wife what you saw. You couldn't bring yourself to make her afraid again. You wish you had.

She must have gotten up in the night to use the bathroom. Semiconscious, she turned out the light before returning to bed.

You felt something at the foot of your bed. You heard it breathing like a sickly whine; raspy and otherworldly.

Out of the darkness, it held up a single digit and grabbed for her feet. She screamed for only a moment before it tore out her throat. It looked like a stick figure, looming in the darkness. Its wicked head turned to you and it held up two digits before smiling, before receding into nothingness along with the body of your wife.

Alone, you shivered and cried until the sun blanketed the horizon. Nothing remained, not even the slightest sign that it had ever been. With your legs drawn up into your chest, you quivered like a lamb, afraid to make the slightest move. Your stomach lurched in on itself and your tongue tingled in fear; swollen and dry.

Once the morning sun had enveloped the sky, you gave the entity a name. You called out in anger and fear. You cursed its existence and swore to its demise. Brave words for a man bathed in the light of a dawning day.

In a state of exhausted dread, you waited out the day, never moving from the spot on your bed where the thing had come and raped away the memory of your love. When darkness came and the sun draped a hue of purple and pink across the skyline, you waited and watched.

You bide your time until the shadow returns.

The house begins to creak as the temperature drops. Like music to vile and wretched things, the shifting house plays its unsettling tune. A penetrating cold rustles through every room, making you shiver as the shadows dance about the walls. Grinding whispers spray out along the floorboards, beckoning you deeper into horror and angst.

A face, silhouetted in darkness, leisurely cocks in from around the door frame of the bedroom. For a brief second, it raises its brow and is gone. Your courage is faltering, waning in the silence. Fear grips at your soul as your skin begins to crawl.

Again, the face peers in. It holds up two digits, long and sickly like twigs from a haunted tree. It laughs in a low rasp which sends a shiver down through your bones. Your body convulses in fear as it suddenly appears at the foot of your bed.

It towers above you, swaying like a blade of grass at the cusp of a storm. Its silence is penetrating. With a length of tongue like a bullwhip, it laps at your flesh. Thick mucus clings to your skin. Its breath is filled with rot and gore like the odor of burning hair and vomit. For a moment, its face transforms into the terror stricken visage of your wife before wiping away into a bottomless open maw.

Its pencil like fingers wrap themselves around your face as it pulls you closer to its cavernous mouth.

It has been said that your life flashes before your eyes at the moment of death. Those who have said such things must never have experienced something as wretched as this.

R. M. Cochran *has been previously published in Holiday of the Dead by Wild Wolf Publishing, Signals from the Void by Rainstorm Press, Collaboration of the Dead presents: Putrid Poetry & Sickening Sketches, and Code Z by Knightwatch Press. His work can also be found in upcoming anthologies such as Technicolor Terror, and the New Flesh Bizarro Anthology.*

Peter, Peter Pumpkin Eater
By S.J. Caunt

Peter, Peter pumpkin eater,
Had a wife but couldn't keep her;
He put her in a pumpkin shell
And there he kept her very well.

Kyle was lost; he'd been wandering through the woods for what seemed like hours now. He sighed in defeat and looked at the ground. Every path he came across looked just the same as the last. His brother, Shawn, was meant to be looking after him but he (and his dumb-ass friend Carl) had run off leaving him alone. It wasn't fair. His mom had made Shawn promise to take him Trick-or-Treating and, although Shawn had moaned, pulled faces, and kicked the kitchen table, he'd finally agreed to look after his younger brother and take him around the estate. Kyle should've known his brother wouldn't keep his word. They'd rung the door bells of about five flats before Shawn grabbed Kyle's pail of sweets and ran off (with Carl lumbering behind) across the road to the common beyond. They'd both jeered and taunted Kyle, swinging his pail of sweets and pretending to eat them. Kyle ran after them, his ghost outfit flapping around him in the evening breeze, but by the time he got to the edge of the woods, they had disappeared. He hated Shawn sometimes (he could be a complete jerk!) but now he just wished he could find him and get home. It was going to be dark soon and spending the night lost and alone in these woods made him shiver. He was trying to be brave, but deep down he was beginning to panic. Kyle wasn't even bothered about the sweets anymore; all he wanted was to get home to his mom.

Kyle called out for his brother again. He was hoping that Shawn and Carl were getting bored from hiding. He'd rather have the embarrassment of screaming like a baby as they jumped out to frighten him than be lost in the woods any longer. It just wasn't funny! He decided to give it a few more minutes (and go a little bit deeper through the trees) before trying to retrace his steps back. As he turned a sharp corner in the path he came to an abrupt stop; a gated wall blocked his route. It was almost waist high and speckled with patches of moss. Beyond the gate he could see a cottage. He nearly punched the air with relief; the owner was bound to have a phone! He could ring his mom and she could come and get him. Shawn would get no tea and probably have his Xbox confiscated for at least a month! It would serve him right for playing such a stupid prank. His brother had ruined Halloween this year.

The cottage was a strange shape; curved around the rooftop with circular windows that looked like pennies. It was the color of sunset and was ridged with furrows along its sides. Weird! Kyle unlatched the gate and entered the garden. He found a massive tangle of vegetables and vines that stretched out all across the garden. There were thick roots criss-crossed all over the cobbled path that led up to the front door and a faint mist had started to swirl around the soles of his shoes. Cautiously he made his way up to the porch and knocked on the pale wooden door.

"Hello? Is there anybody there? Shawn? Carl?" There was no answer. "SHAWN????" Where was he? There had to be someone home (he could see a faint glow inside through one of the small windows). He pushed at the door and to his surprise it slowly creaked open. Surely it wouldn't hurt to have a quick look around for a phone would it? He entered cautiously and found himself in a room full of pumpkins. The person that lived here was a fan of Halloween he thought, probably even more so than me!

"Excuse me. Hello? I just need to use the phone." Kyle scanned the room around him. There didn't seem to be anybody home so he ventured further into the orangey gloom. He noticed that a couple of the pumpkins were lit, their glowing faces casting shadows up the wall as the light outside began to fade. He approached them; his eyes darting around nervously as he looked for the phone. The faces that had been carved into them were eerie; mouths had been hacked-out in an almost scream-like grimace and the haunted eyes staring back at Kyle made him shudder. Maybe he should go back outside and try to get home on his own...

"What are you doing young man?" A female voice behind him asked. He spun around and peered toward the open door. "Or girl...I can't make out what you are with that sheet over your head."

"I'm sorry...I'm Kyle. I've lost my brother and his friend. We were Trick-or-Treating, but they ran off into the woods and now I'm lost. The door was open and I was just looking for a phone." Kyle spurted out. "I haven't touched anything, I promise. Please can I phone my mom to come and get me?"

"Lost are we little ghost-ling?" The woman shuffled closer toward Kyle. "Left all alone in the woods, eh? Need a phone to call your mommy?" A faint giggle rose from her direction.

Kyle suddenly felt uneasy and began to back away from the woman. He couldn't make out her face properly through the eye slits of his ghost costume, but something about her made him feel icy cold. He backed into something, knocking it over with his heel. He spun around quickly and noticed he'd upset a pail of sweets; *his* pail of sweets! He turned to face the figure.

"My brother's been here! Where...is...he?" Kyle tried not to sound frightened, but his words came out stuttered. Panic began to swell up inside of him and he started to tremble.

"You mean that rude boy and his friend? I caught them rummaging through my things. One of them was your brother? Oh my! Fancy that indeed!" She approached slowly, her movements stooped and jittery. "Don't worry my little ghost. Your brother is here. Indeed he is!"

Kyle clenched his fists and chewed his bottom lip as the woman stepped into the orange glow of light cast by the pumpkins. Finally he saw her face; a contorted mask of fleshy pulp that hung within a frizz of hair. Her eyes were white and large and blinked heavily as she stared manically at Kyle.

"Why your brother and his friend are just behind you my little ghost. See how *he* glows. See how well *they* turned out!"

Kyle looked over his shoulder. His eyes widened as his gaze fell onto the two crudely etched faces of the lit pumpkins. No, he thought; surely that wasn't his brother staring back at him with eyes like fire? How could that be?

"And now my dear it's time for *you* to join your brother. Break into my house will you? Try to steal my things will you? Think there isn't a price to pay for such thievery do you? There's *always* a price to pay little ghost!"

Kyle went to run for the door, but the woman threw up her arms. Two knotted husks of what looked like roots slammed against the sides of the house blocking his escape route. Her 'arms' embedded themselves into the soft tissue of the walls. The room quivered and Kyle suddenly realized that it wasn't a house at all; he was trapped inside a giant pumpkin! He shuffled backwards, crunching the sweets underfoot. Suddenly, all the pumpkins in the room flared up, their lit innards illuminating the full horror of the creature before him. The carved-out mouths screamed and Kyle put his hands up to his ears. He couldn't block out the cries of their pain no matter how hard he pushed. The creature threw back her sagging face and laughed. From her torso shot several vines; they grabbed Kyle by the feet and knocked him off balance. His screams joined that of the others trapped in the room as he was dragged along the floor to meet his end.

"Don't worry my little ghost. Soon you'll join the rest of my children this All Hallows Eve. Oh yes indeed! But first I need to plant you, plant you deep in the dirt so you can grow and be reborn. You'll soon be *the* perfect Jack-O-Lantern. Oh yes indeed! And the face...the face! I'll carve you out a face that will make even the most hellish of hearts tremble in fear!"

And with that Kyle disappeared into the soil like a ghost evaporating into the night...

I'm a UK based children's and YA bookseller and confirmed book addict! I was raised on a diet of horror films and all things that go bump in the night. I live for Halloween (but dread Christmas) and every October I search the local store for the biggest pumpkins, sharpen my knives, and carve out the best Jack-O-Lanterns on my street! I'm currently working on my first YA novel which will (obviously) be full of gore, frights, and dead things!

The Journey Home
By Shawn M. Riddle

Anne's heart was racing, now was the time. After being trapped in her office building for two hours since the outbreak began, she couldn't delay another minute. Her daughter Allie was at home--she had locked herself in the basement on Anne's instructions. Now Anne had to reach her fast.

The virus, or whatever had caused the dead to return to life hit the city like a bomb. Almost immediately, thousands of creatures were running through the streets, attacking, killing, and spreading the condition to others. Many of her co-workers tried to leave the building. Most, if not all, who had tried had failed. They were attacked and mauled right outside the doors and the surviving few, including herself retreated and hid in a fourth floor office. When she told the others she was leaving to get her daughter, they tried to convince her to stay--begged her even. But she couldn't-- nothing was going to keep her from her little girl, not even those monsters. Despite their protests, she left the office and made her way to the underground parking garage through the stairwell.

Her breath quickened as she took her van keys and a .380 pistol from her purse. She peeked out the door of the garage foyer into the large parking area. It seemed to be clear and quiet. Taking a few deep breaths and steeling herself, she inched the door open and began to make her way to her van, about 150 feet from the foyer. She moved quickly and quietly, scanning in all directions as she moved.

She was no more than fifty feet from her van when a high-pitched feral shriek and the sounds of fast moving footfalls echoed through the garage. She looked to her right and saw one of the creatures running toward her. It snarled and shrieked as it ran. Blood flowed from a gaping wound in its neck. She turned, raised her pistol, and pulled the trigger; her first shot went wild, missing the charging creature. She held her breath and squeezed off a well-aimed second shot, blowing a hole right through the creature's left eye. It dropped to the ground twitching at her feet.

She continued on to the van, using the remote to unlock it as she ran and jumped in. Her hands shook as she slid they key into the ignition. She backed the van up and started for the exit, running over the body of her attacker on the way out for good measure. As she turned onto the city street, the van's engine began to rev higher and the van slowed, her transmission had slipped, and she was going nowhere fast. "Come on, not now!" she screamed as she slammed her fist onto the steering wheel. As if obeying her command, the transmission slipped back into gear and the van lurched forward violently. She only had one hand on the wheel when the van took off and she lost control for a moment, scraping a concrete light pole on the side of the road, knocking off her side mirror and leaving a huge scrape on the side of the van. She sped down the road, swerving constantly to avoid wrecked cars, debris and people in the road. She couldn't tell if more people were living or dead, but at this moment she didn't care. Her only thoughts were of getting home to her daughter.

On more than one occasion, she had to drive on the sidewalk to get past reefs of wrecked and burning cars. As she turned onto Parsons Street, slammed her brakes and came to a screeching halt. The road was completely filled with the creatures. Hundreds of them dotted the streets, attacking and killing what few people remained. They spotted her van and shrieked in unison, the sound akin to an old air raid siren. They charged straight at her. Not even thinking she slammed her foot down on the gas pedal and barreled straight into the running horde.

She screamed as she pressed the pedal to the floor, running into dozens of the creatures and knocking them out of her way. Several of them hit the windshield as she mowed through them, cracking the glass and leaving streaks of blood and bits of hair on the glass. She could hear their bones break as she rolled over them, the shrieking now at a deafening volume. One of the creatures got stuck in the front wheel well as she ran it over, bringing the van to another halt. The creatures beat against the glass and metal of the van on all sides and the vehicle was rocked from side to side. She grabbed the gear shift and threw the van into reverse, freeing the body that was caught underneath. She turned slightly to the right and floored the gas pedal again until she plowed through to the other side of the horde. She sped down the street, and continued toward home.

After the longest ten minutes of her life, she pulled onto her street. There was less activity here than she encountered on her way home, but it was by no means clear. She pulled up in front of her house and parked the battered van in front. She left the engine running as she separated her house keys from the rest and darted for the front door. Two creatures ran around the side of the house, making a beeline for her. Without hesitating she shot both as she ran. Both dropped to the ground. *Thank God Michael taught me to use this thing* she thought as she unlocked her front door and ran into the house. She slammed the door behind her and ran to the basement door.

"Allie! Are you here baby? It's mommy," she yelled as she hammered on the basement door. She heard a small voice on the other side.

"Mom! I'm down here," Allie said. Anne could hear her footsteps as she ran up the stairs and opened the door.

Anne grabbed her daughter and hugged her tight, tears flowing from her eyes like rain.

"Mom, I'm scared. What's happening?" Allie cried.

"I don't know baby, but it's not safe here. We have to leave."

"No! I don't want to go out there, there're monsters out there and they're hurting people."

"I know baby, but we have to get somewhere safe, okay?"

She pulled back slightly from her mother and nodded. "Where's Dad?"

"I don't know baby, we'll find him, but we have to leave now before more of *them* come."

Anne turned to her daughter, "Stay right behind me, and don't move unless I tell you to, OK?" Allie nodded, terror and apprehension written on her face. Anne readied her pistol and threw the front door open just as a group of three creatures came running up the walkway. She shielded her daughter with her body as she shot the creatures. The slide locked back on her pistol as the last creature fell.

She stuffed the gun into her pocket and grabbed her daughter's hand tightly as she raced to the van. She made her way around the side and saw at least a dozen more creatures running her way. At that same moment, a large army truck turned the corner onto the street, running into the pack of creatures and sending most of them flying. The surviving few creatures broke off their run toward the girls and headed for the truck. Machine gun fire erupted from the passenger and driver's side of the truck, dropping the creatures as they ran.

A man in uniform jumped out of the truck and called to the girls, "Anne! Allie!" They raced over to him, and hugged him tight.

Allie screamed, "Daddy!"

Anne kissed her husband and said, "Michael, thank God, thank God, what's happening?"

"I don't know for sure honey, but it's everywhere, we have to get out of here. Get in, we're going to the base. We can use one of the old fallout shelters for now."

They held their embrace for a moment longer, then jumped in the truck and sped off toward the base. Their fate uncertain, but their spirits were high. Whatever happened, they would be together.

Shawn M. Riddle *is from the Northern Virginia area, just outside Washington D.C. He currently works as a construction Quality Assurance Engineer. He grew up on a steady diet of George A. Romero and slasher movies. He is also currently working on his first novel in the Zombie genre. He runs a fan group for author David Moody on Facebook and can be found there as Shawn 'Rotting Corpse' Riddle.*

The Bully Minder
By S. S. Michaels

What did you say? My daughter has a boy's name? Listen, you might want to lay off of her. And, not just because I think you're a couple of snot-nosed little brats. My kids, you see, they have a protector, a kind of body guard. And he already knows your names.

Late at night, after you and your parents are all tucked nice and snug into your little beds, he watches you. From the sidewalk in front of your house. People driving by think he's just a guy walking his dog. They drive by him in the dark, on their way home from the movies or maybe a basketball game. Sometimes they even wave to him, like they do every other neighbor around here. Who knows, maybe they already know who he is. Maybe he's waiting for them, just like he's waiting for you.

This guy, he isn't just some ordinary man, though. He's an angel. Not the kind of angel who has beautiful wings and sings praise to God. He's the kind that was cast down from Heaven and holds the hand of the devil. He's the kind of angel you really don't want watching over you. And he does watch over you. You know that shadow you see in the corner of your room sometimes, when you wake up in the middle of the night because you think you want a drink of water? Yeah, well, it might not be just a shadow.

Why you, you ask? Because you come onto my street and tell my daughter that she has a boy's name, you take her friend's toys and heat up his face with embarrassment and shame. And from the very first time you picked on my little ones, our angel showed up in front of your house. Only you didn't know it because you were asleep.

See, he knows the ones who pick on the little kids, the ones who push them down and call them names. He has all bullies' names written on his black heart and they – *you* -- belong to him. That's right. The first time you say a bad word, he will smile. The first time you lay your hands on another child, he will laugh with delight. I bet you've done those things already. You bet he knows your name.

Know what he does? He waits for night from the woods behind your house. He drinks from the stinking creek and flicks his smoldering cigarette butts in the mud. He watches you and your family cut the grass and blow bubbles in the back yard. Whenever you go near the creek, when the sun is high in the sky, he sinks just below the surface. If you look closely, and the creek's not too muddy, you might see the top of his head, his greasy black hair floating near the top of the water, or a couple of bubbles. But don't get too close – he can smell you. Sometimes, when you're close, he wonders what you'll taste like.

What happens is this: He picks out the bullies in the neighborhood, and he watches them. And he waits. At night, when he's out in front of your house with his dog-creature, he's counting the minutes until you'll be with him in the big White Room that is neither Heaven nor Hell but somewhere in between. His dog-thing sits next to him, stomach rumbling, drool running from his lips in fat strings. When the sun starts coming up, they'll slip around to the back of your house and take their place next to the creek.

Wherever you move, whichever college you go to, wherever you live when you grow up, he will be there, watching you, minding you. When you are thirty years old, sitting behind your desk, working at your soul-sucking accounting job or whatever you've fallen into, thinking to yourself what a crummy life you've got, just remember: things are going to get a lot worse when you die. He'll be there. He won't forget.

When you die, he'll take you to the White Room. It's where all the bullies go. You'll do the waiting, then. You'll see that his dog really isn't a dog at all – its mouth is just a little too wide, its fur a little too thick, and its eyes just a little too human. And you'll smell them, the fallen angel and his dog-thing. You will gag on the stench. You and the other bullies will be so scared you'll be peeing in your pants. And, of course, the other bullies, watching the dark stain spread across the front of your pants, will laugh at you, because, after all, that's what bullies do.

And he will take you. The angel, the Bully Minder. One by one, the other bullies will disappear into what you think is a closet, holding his bony hand. You won't know what happens in the closet until it's your turn.

And your turn will come.

I know what happens.

The Bully Minder will turn to face you and he will clear his throat. He will open his mouth, unhinging it like a snake, and his pointed teeth will rip the mouth right off your face so you can't scream. He will laugh at you, push you down, tell you that you have a sissy name and need a diaper. Then he will look deep into your wide eyes, smiling his horrible smile. You'll try to look away, but you won't be able to. He will drink your soul right out of your eyeballs. When your body is completely empty and he's full of your spirit, he will feed your shell to his stinking dog-thing, who will gobble you up with the most horrible bone-cracking lip-smacking noises you could imagine.

And he'll go back down Walthour Road, over the creek, to Captain John's Drive, searching for other bullies to fill the empty space you will leave.

So, you see, it's really in your best interest to stay away from my kids and their pals. They are friends with the Bully Minder. He watches over them like a guardian angel. He loves them.

He'll be back to watch you tonight. Count on it. You're already in his heart. And it's Halloween – his favorite.

Have fun trick-or-treating, Batman and Cinderella!

And, what was that you were saying about my daughter's name?

S. S. Michaels *is a writer of transgressive fiction, with several novels on submission and two anthologies in the works. She has lived abroad, traveled widely, jumped out of an airplane and driven a race car. She has worked in film and television for such organizations as Ridley Scott's Scott Free, dick clark productions, inc., and CBS. She lives on the Georgia coast with her husband, two kids, two dogs, and a swarm of unfriendly sand gnats.*

Something is Out There
By Nathan Correll

A fat moon sat high in the crisp October night. Heavy dew, which would be frost by morning, covered the grass on the side of the road and clung delicately to the stalks of corn that were left standing in the fields. An old John Deere combine sat vacant near the woods at the far side of a half-harvested field; its driver had left the door open. Carl drove down the road listening to "Stairway to Heaven". In the passenger seat Stacy lit a cigarette and took a long drag.

"This is the best part!" Carl tapped his fingers on the steering wheel to the music and started singing in a high-pitched tone. Stacy rolled her eyes and took another drag from her cigarette.

In the backseat, Shelly slid across the cold vinyl and kissed Lenny on the neck. He barely noticed as he stared out the window at the approaching fields. His breath fogged up the glass.

"Are you ok?" She rubbed her hand on his knee.

"Huh?"

"Well, you've barely said a word since we left the party." She kissed him on the mouth; he could taste vodka.

"I'm fine." He looked back out the window. "I just don't like this kind of thing." He straightened the collar of his jacket.

"Are you still pissing and moaning about this?" Carl said as he turned down the radio. Blue Oyster Cult had started up and Lenny found the cowbell annoying.

"I'm not 'pissing and moaning' about anything. I just think this it's dumb."

"It's Halloween. Lighten up! Live a little!" Carl adjusted the rearview mirror and smiled at his friend. Lenny didn't smile back.

"You're not really scared are you?" Shelly poked at his side with her finger and he jumped.

"I'm not scared! I'd just rather be back at the party. Drinking." He tried to smile.

Stacy spun around from the front seat and took another long drag. "I'm with you, Lenny. This is lame."

They drove on down the road which went from blacktop, to gravel, to dirt. There were cornfields on all sides. The corn looked sharp and jagged against the moonlit sky. In each field the moon illuminated the scarecrows standing guard. Their heads hung down toward the earth, arms outstretched in tattered rags. From their wooden poles above the field they seemed to watch through cross-stitched eyes as the car drove by; threatening to leap down and chase them. He imagined their burlap faces were jagged with crooked teeth like an evil jack-o-lantern. Lenny felt sweat beading on his forehead. He looked away from the fields.

The road became bumpy and the 1977 powder blue Lincoln bounced with each groove as they rounded a sharp turn and slowed down. The headlights caught a break in the fields of corn. The car pulled into a gravel driveway and slowed to a stop. Shelly and Lenny leaned forward from the back seat to peer at the rusted sign arched above the driveway: "Gatlin-Myers Cemetery."

Carl smiled at Stacy like a kid on Christmas morning. She rolled her eyes at him again. Why the hell did her boyfriend get off on this shit? She had been to more than her fair share of "haunted" places. She dug around in her purse and pulled out a shiny flask. She unscrewed the cap and took a drink. "Anyone else?" Carl opened the car door with a squeak and stepped outside. The others followed.

The cemetery was situated in the middle of two fields of corn. The scarecrows watched. It was a large cemetery surrounded by a wrought-iron fence; tarnished spikes adorned the top of each bar. Toward the back was an old building that at one time had housed the caretaker. The windows were mostly busted out and the roof sagged with the age of many years. The wind rattled through the corn; the tin roof screamed. Several Oak trees populated the grounds; their old branches stretched far into the sky, their roots cracked through the surface of the ground like veins.

Two stone columns held the main gate in place. A gargoyle was mounted on top of each column, watching. Their wings were folded behind their back and their teeth were bared. Lenny shivered.

"Let's go." Carl walked to the gate; Shelly was right behind him while Lenny lagged behind mulling about. Stacy lit another cigarette and leaned against the hood of the car.

"Wait." Lenny's voice cracked. "You know those kids died up here, right?"

"You aren't serious are you? I mean, you don't really believe that, do you?" Carl rattled the gate.

"Don't you? If you don't then why are we out here?"

"Because it's Halloween." Carl laughed.

"They found them in pieces. My dad told me so."

"Yeah, Lenny, I know the story. They found the kids scattered in pieces from here to the shed back there and the only other thing they found was the arm of a scarecrow. Ooooooooo." He clapped his hands together and Lenny jumped.

"It's kid's stuff." He opened the gate. "You guys coming or what?" He looked at the others. Shelly nodded eagerly.

"Eh, what the hell?" Stacy took a swig from her flask and shrugged her shoulders. She hopped off the hood and followed the other two through the gate.

"You coming with us or you want to sit in the car?" Craig raised an eyebrow at Lenny.

Carl looked at Shelly who batted her eyes at him. "Please." She begged.

"Fine." He finally agreed with reluctance. Somewhere in the distance a crow called out. The wind stirred the corn and tin roof moaned in defiance. "But let's make it quick."

The group made their way through the cemetery toward the shed in the back. Some of the headstones were huge and ornate. They were old too, some dating back to the 1700's and some so old that the writing had completely worn off. They were almost to the shed when Lenny stopped.

"Did you hear that?" The others turned to face him. The wind blew in a gust and kicked dirt from the ground.

"Now who's the funny man?" Carl smirked at his friend.

"I'm serious. It sounded like something's in the field." They all listened. There was a rustling in the corn. Shelly cuddled up to Lenny.

"It's probably a deer or something." Carl tried to get them moving. "I want to see what's inside the shed." Again there was a noise from the field. It was closer. It was coming down the row of corn.

"I'm going back to the car." Lenny grabbed Shelly's arm. "You're going with me." There was a noise again. It was just beyond the fence on the other side. It seemed to be coming from all around them.

"Are you kidding me?" Carl was clearly agitated. "Don't be such a baby!" He yelled, but Lenny and Shelly were already headed toward the car. "You won't get far without these." He dangled the car keys in the air. They stopped.

In the field something stirred. Stacy stared straight ahead in the dark and tried to adjust her eyes. Something was wrong. She dropped her cigarette and took a step back. "Someone is out there." Gooseflesh raced across her arms.

"Don't be stupid. There isn't anyone out there. There's no one out here but us!" Stacy turned away from Carl.

Again, there was a rustling in the field and this time Carl heard it; he heard it all around them. "What the hell is that?" From the corner of his eye, near the old shed, he saw a shadow move. His heart sank to his feet and panic filled his head. "Let's get out of here!"

They were running; sprinting. Something was behind them. Lenny turned to catch a glimpse and felt something on his foot. He looked down and saw the root of a giant oak tree as he toppled over and banged his head against a tombstone. The pain was sharp and instant; blood trickled from his forehead into his eye. He heard screaming and then everything went black.

When he woke up the sun was out. He was lying on a stretcher behind an ambulance. He could see police cars parked on both sides of the road. Across the cemetery gates was bright yellow police tape. He watched as uniformed men carried black bags from the cemetery. Somewhere in the background he could hear a woman crying. He closed his eyes and tried not to think. The scarecrows were watching. Smiling.

Nathan Correll *resides in Charleston, South Carolina. He is a graduate of Southern Illinois University - Carbondale with a major in Television Production and a minor in Creative Writing. As a longtime horror enthusiast he enjoys writing both fiction and poetry and is currently working on his first full-length novel. Nathan loves hearing from people who enjoy his stories. Feel free to reach him at n.c.correll@gmail.com.*

The Licked Hand
By Mark Goddard

As she waved goodbye to her parents and closed the front door Nancy Blake sighed with relief. She had waited three whole months for Halloween to come around so she could have some time alone and now, she had the whole weekend to get the booze flowing, some gory films in the DVD player and her girls over to celebrate the weekend in blood soaked style. Nancy loved Halloween, her Dad had brought her up on Hammer horror films ever since see was ten years old. Her parents always spent the Halloween weekend at her Dad's brother's for a huge Halloween party, but this year Nancy just wanted a quiet night with her friends. But that was tomorrow night; tonight was her night to relax.

Nancy trudged into the kitchen. She grabbed a bottle of water from the fridge, along with the other half of a sandwich she had left at lunch. Ham and pickle. She looked at the sandwich lovingly and took a massive bite. "Mmm, tasty," she said to herself as she headed through the hallway and into the living room. She slumped herself down on the sofa and grabbed the remote. In the corner of the room, her dog Charlie looked up at her, his eyes still full of slumber. He laid back down, his tail wagging. Nancy picked up the remote from the arm of the sofa and turn on the television.

She flicked through the channels and past *Eastenders* and the tripe they were showing on BBC Three. Another show with drunken teenagers throwing their guts up in the streets of a clubbing hotspot. As she continued to skip through the many pointless Freeview channels, she finally stopped on the BBC news. She lay down on the sofa dramatically and looked over at Charlie.

"I'm so bloody bored Charlie," she complained. Charlie got up and plodded over to her licking her hand which was dangling over the arm of the sofa. The news finished talking about the war in Libya and went to the local news *Look East*. A middle aged woman appeared on the screen.

"*Good evening and welcome to Look East. There have been reports of a murderer on the loose in Colchester tonight. Over the past 2 weeks the bodies of three young girls have been found brutally murdered in their homes.*

Police ask that anyone taking their children trick-or-treating tonight should...."

Nancy sat up and quickly turned the channel over to a far less depressing E4, where *Friends* was being shown again for the five hundredth time. She stroked Charlie's head and drifted into sleep.

The sound of a car door slamming shut made Nancy wake up with a start. E4 had now moved on from *Friends* and was now playing the horror film *28 Days Later*. Charlie bolted up and ran into the kitchen. Nancy sat up. It must be trick-or-treaters TP-ing the neighbor's car again. Charlie was whimpering in the hallway. She got up and headed into the kitchen. She walked through the hall, bent down and cuddled the scared dog. "Oh Charlie you big silly, there is nothing in there." Nancy walked into the kitchen and turned on the light. Outside the rain had started to fall and a wind was picking up.

"See you silly thing," she said as she walked over to the sink. She grabbed a glass and filled it with water. That was when she noticed the door was ajar. "See? That was what you heard, Charlie." Nancy locked the door and bolted it at the top and the bottom. She made her way around the house checking every window and door. The news had got under her skin a little. The thought of a killer on the loose made her goosepimply. She made her way upstairs and checked the upper floor windows and headed to her bedroom. Charlie ran under the bed, his usual place, and laid down. Nancy took off her clothes and walked over to the closet. She was about to open the wardrobe door when a loud bang form outside made Charlie start whimpering again. She walked over to the window. The wind had blown a recycling bin over. She watched as it got stuck under the wheels of a car parked outside the neighbor's house.

"Oh Charlie, don't be such a wimp."

Dumping her clothes on the floor, she went to the wardrobe and took out an old t-shirt and shorts. She got changed and got into bed. She put her hand outside the covers and let her hand dangle at the side of the bed. Charlie started licking her hand. She drifted off into sleep.

At 2:00AM, Nancy woke up. The house was dark but at least the wind and rain had died down. She could hear a dripping sound. "Argh freaking piping," she complained as she got out of bed and into the bathroom. She checked the taps were off and headed back to bed. She put her hand at the side of the bed again. She felt the wetness of Charlie's tongue against her hand again and closed her eyes. Still the dripping continued.

DRIP. DRIP.DRIP

This time the dripping sounded closer, like the water was hitting wood. She looked up toward to roof. "Ah for god sake, the roof can't be leaking," she complained out loud. She got out of bed and walked out onto the landing. The dripping continued, but it seemed like it coming from behind her. She headed back into the bedroom, stopped still and listened. The noise was coming from the wardrobe. Cautiously, she walked toward it, her hand clammy, sweat formed on the forehead. She opened the door and screamed. In the wardrobe, hanging from a length of garden hosepipe was Charlie, his face had been sliced off and his chest had been cut open. The dog's guts had dropped on to the floor of the wardrobe. Nancy covered her mouth and started to back out of the room. She turned on the bedroom light and screamed as she saw the writing in blood above her bed.

HUMANS CAN LICK TOO

From under the bed crawled a middle aged man, dripping wet from the evening's rain, a knife in his hand. He wore an old sandy colored army camouflage uniform covered in a mixture of fresh and dried blood. On his face, the man was wearing the freshly flayed face of Charlie as a mask. The man's breathing was heavy as he got to his feet. The man's breathing was like the breathing of a dog. Nancy bolted for the bathroom. The dog masked man was close behind her; his sicken chuckle echoed through the silent hallway. Nancy rushed into the bathroom and slammed the door shut just as the dog masked man slammed his knife into it. She locked the bathroom door and back slowly up against the wall. The dog masked man fell onto all fours and started scrapping at the door with his dirty nails, before slamming his whole body against it. The man howled as he continued to attack the door. Nancy screamed with every attempt he tried. Amongst the confusion, Nancy could hear another dripping sound coming from behind the shower curtain. Slowly she got to her feet and reached carefully for the shower curtain. She pulled them open and screamed. Hanging from the shower curtain rail were her parents.

The door burst open. The dog faced man howled. Nancy

screamed.

Born in raised by the sea in Essex in the UK **Mark Goddard** *is a young horror writer who lives and breathes the horror genre. Mark runs the horror review and interview website Snakebite Horror and Reviews for the Film4 Frightfest website. On Halloween in 2009 Mark co-released horror film trivia book THE HORROR FILM QUIZ BOOK and has had a short published in Film4 FrightFest's online e-Magazine. A former bookseller for Waterstone's he lives alone typing away in the hope to entertain horror fans with his gruesome tales.*

Chewy Ones
By Jeff Szpirglas

"Do I have to?" Alain whined, like he did every Halloween.

The response was swift and firm. "Now, please."

Alain rolled his eyes and slung the bag onto the kitchen table. A sea of colorful, cellophane-wrapped gems spilled out. Alain had filled a garbage bag with candy this year. The thing weighed a ton. He felt like Santa Claus on Christmas Eve, only this bag was full of candy, and it was ALL HIS.

At least, until Mom and Dad finished picking through it.

In a moment, Alain's parents were spreading the candies across the table, filling every bit of free space. They were obsessed with checking each one to make sure that the candies, chocolates, chips, and whatever else he'd gathered were not poisoned, tainted, or had concealed bits of wire or razor blades.

Alain was no dummy. He knew good candy from bad candy. But all he could do was stand and tap his foot impatiently as Mom and Dad sorted his loot into the Good and Bad piles.

It was like watching the quality control people on factory assembly lines. They stooped over the table, plucking out suspiciously-wrapped tidbits and eyeing them under the kitchen light above. "Nope," Dad said firmly, and tossed a loosely-wrapped chocolate into the garbage.

"Not this one, either," Mom snapped a second later, and flung away a toffee with a slight bend in it.

"This will stick to your molars. I bet you a dentist handed it out."

"I read a study saying this brand of potato chip causes brain damage."

"And this candy wrapper has been shown to make laboratory mice disobedient."

They continued tirelessly for a half hour. Mom and Dad had already gone through his kid sister Jacqueline's treats. She ended up losing one third of her haul to the garbage. All Alain could do was look on as his efforts were whittled away piece by piece.

"What's this?" Mom asked, picking out a tightly-wrapped object.

It was round, maybe a chocolate or a gumball. The packaging was some sort of bright foil, a mixture of every color that Alain had ever seen. As Mom rolled it in her open palm, the wrapper caught the kitchen light and reflected it into Alain's eyes. It was mesmerizing to stare at. It made the kitchen start to spin so delightfully.

Alain reached out, not to eat it, just to touch it.

Seeing this, Mom snatched it away. "Not this one, either, I'm afraid." She closed her palm so that Alain could not see the wrapper. Alain blinked once. Twice. His head cleared. "Why not?"

"I don't like the look of it," she admitted.

Alain jabbed a finger at her. "You don't like the look of anything!" he snapped. "You ruin Halloween, that's what you do!"

Dad sidled sternly into view. "Alain, we're only doing this to keep you safe. Haven't you heard about what happens if you don't check your candy?"

"Yeah, you *enjoy* it!"

"That's it. Go to your room."

Alain was already thumping up the stairs. He slammed the door, sat down on his bed, and fumed.

* * *

Later that night, when his parents were asleep, Alain's eyes snapped open.

He'd been dreaming, but not the usual sort. This one was just colors, like the kind he'd seen on that amazing wrapper.

Alain slipped out of bed, out of his room, and tiptoed downstairs. He used the shaft of moonlight slanting in through the window to see. He didn't need to eat the candy, just to see that wrapper again.

Once he got to the kitchen, Alain pulled open the drawer underneath the sink, and peered into the garbage. He reached into his pocket and pulled out the small flashlight he'd brought from upstairs. He shone it into the garbage. It was a disgusting mix of candies and table scraps.

Alain plunged his hand in there and stirred the garbage. He pulled his slimy hand out, wiped it off on his pajamas, and then shone the light back into the can. A burst of color shimmered back at him. Alain smiled as the world around him dimmed, and all he could take in was the light.

Alain plucked out the round candy. The colors shifted like the skin of a chameleon.

He had to have that wrapper for himself!

He peeled a corner off, revealing a dull white candy underneath. Alain took extra special care to peel the foil without tearing it. Soon he got it off and spread it into a square. Then he noticed the smell.

It was coming from the candy. Like the wrapper, the smell kept changing. First, he caught a whiff of cotton candy. Next, licorice. After that, a marshmallow odor. Alain was already salivating.

He knew better than to put things in his mouth that had been in the garbage. But it was wrapped in foil. There was no way any germs were on it. Besides, what could one little candy do?

Alain popped it into his mouth.

At once, his tongue went into taste spasms. The candy danced from flavor to flavor. His senses had never experienced anything like this. He wanted to, but could not savor it. Alain chomped down.

It was so chewy. Almost like a piece of gum. And the chewy ones were THE BEST.

Each bite made him salivate more, and each swallow was a different delicious flavor.

It was almost too much, in fact. Soon Alain's sense of smell and taste were so overpowered by the chewy morsel that he needed to take a breather. He stood up and paced to the kitchen window. Pushing it open, Alain took a deep breath, and stared into the night sky.

A stretch of clouds blanketed the full moon. There were other things in the sky as well. Airplanes, most likely, so high up that all Alain could see were ant-sized pinpricks above.

Alain kept chewing. The taste was amazing, but it really was getting to be too much. He opened his mouth to spit out the candy, but it wouldn't leave.

Alain formed his lips into an O-shaped circle and tried to force the candy out.

It wouldn't budge.

The more he strained, the more the candy resisted. Alain took a deep breath and blew hard. But the candy changed form. It thinned into a balloon-like substance that bubbled out of his mouth.

Alain tried to pop the bubble. Although thin, it was strong, even when Alain grabbed a knife from the kitchen to stab it. Alain kept jabbing at it, but the bubble would not pop.

Because he couldn't use his mouth, Alain began to panic. He breathed hard. This just made the bubble grow. That gave him an idea. He put the knife down and filled the bubble with more air, hoping it would stretch and burst.

Instead, Alain felt his feet lift away from the floor. He was floating.

He dog-paddled with his arms, just like he'd learned in swimming lessons, but a gust of wind swept in through the open window. It twirled him about, and then sucked him outside.

The current of air was strong. Alain watched in amazed horror as he floated up past the roof, past the big old tree in the backyard. His vision was filled with a birds-eye-view of the neighborhood. How was he going to get down?

He kept floating. Maybe Alain could suck air back into his lungs, deflate it, and float back down. But he'd already pumped too much air into the thing. His lungs would burst.

Looking around, Alain began to notice the objects in the air he'd seen earlier. The sky was dotted with about ten or more other kid-like shapes. Each one had a large bubble sticking out of its mouth.

It was getting colder the further Alain rose. He shivered, partly because of the cold, but mostly because of what he saw next.

Hovering above the floating kids were several other shapes. They were also human, but they were on broomsticks, and they whizzed about the night sky like gleeful fireflies. They all had pointed hats, warty noses, and they were all smiling at him hungrily.

A few had even spread a big, net like object out between them. Alain saw some of the kids float right into the net. They waved their arms wildly. He could hear them trying to scream through the big candy bubbles coming from their mouths.

Alain floated faster. He tried to paddle away, but the net caught him.

As he looked into the big, bright moon, he caught sight of his closest captor, who pointed at him excitedly. "Oh, look! I bet that one's chewy! Don't you know the chewy ones are THE BEST?!"

Jeff Szpirglas knows about gross and scary things, especially after writing the non-fiction books "Gross Universe" and "Fear This Book" (Maple Tree Press). Hailing from Toronto, he has written for radio, television, and yes, even an educational parenting video. He is an avid elementary school teacher, an excitable Dr. Who fan, and a terrible cook. His newest books include "You Just Can't Help It: Your Guide to the Wild and Wacky World of Human Behavior" (Owlkids) and "Something's Fishy" (Orca). Up next is his novel, "Evil Eye," a delightful tale for young readers about a malevolent disembodied human eye.

The Initiation
By Michael C. Dick

Mark cursed silently to himself as he was smacked in the face by the tall, dried corn stalks he was fighting to make his way through.

"Of all the nights to choose from they had to pick Halloween night to initiate new members into their club," he muttered as yet another stalk swung and smacked him in the face.

"This is the stupidest initiation I've ever heard of," he grumbled as he wiped sweat and dirt from his forehead and eyes.

To make matters worse, they wouldn't even allow him to bring a flashlight. His moonlight view quickly faded to dark as menacing clouds covered half the night sky. *Great* he thought, *what's next? Rain?* He should have gone with his original plan and skipped the initiation to go to the Halloween party.

"Where the heck are you?" He asked as if calling to the scarecrow he was sent to find, then retrieve its hat. "If I find it soon, I'll still be able to make it to the party..." A high pitched screech left his mouth as he lost his footing and came crashing to the dirt.

"Of all the lousy luck," he yelled at no one in particular. He struggled to his feet, brushing himself off when suddenly the night was lit up by a series of bright flashes that revealed a large shadowy figure towering over Mark.

Holy Cow!" Mark burst out as the figure came into view again and again with each burst of lightning. "That darn scarecrow scarred me half to death," he said in a shaky voice as he massaged his rapidly beating heart.

"It's a lot taller than I imagined it to be," he said as he started walking again until at last he stood at the base of the scarecrow. Mark tilted his head way back and let out a low drawn out whistle. "This thing has got to be almost ten feet tall. How the heck am I going to get up there?" he wondered out loud.

Scratching his head in bewilderment he walked around the scarecrow until he stood in front of it again. "Well I can only see one way of doing this," Mark said as he reached up and untied the scarecrow's feet from the cross section of wood that they rested on. "Sorry to do this Mr. Scarecrow," Mark joked, "but you seem to be pretty secure with your hands and arms tied to that cross section and I'm afraid I need this one for my feet so if you would be so kind as to move over just a bit." He wrapped his arms around the scarecrows torso pulled himself up.

Once he had his feet balanced on the cross beam he stretched his arms up and over his head trying to reach the hat, but missed it by a good two feet.

"Crud," he cursed as he repositioned himself, wrapped his arms around the scarecrow's torso again and started pulling himself up once more.

Eventually after much grumbling and struggling Mark found himself starring into the face of the scarecrow. "What's a nice guy like you doing in a cornfield like this?" he joked as lightning lit up the night sky again forcing Mark to close his eyes against the brilliant flashes.

As the lightning subsided, Mark opened his eyes and nearly fell from his perch. The scarecrow seemed to stare Mark in the face, looking straight at him and appearing angry. He reached up over his head and grabbed hold of the hat trying to ignore the uneasy feelings he was having.

Much to Mark's surprise, the hat wouldn't budge so he tugged and pulled until finally, with a loud squelching noise, the hat pulled free catching Mark off guard. The force sent Mark unceremoniously to the ground.

Standing up and rubbing his wounded pride, Mark faced the scarecrow and was about to thank him for his generosity when he noticed something odd; the scarecrow's head was starred down at him instead of looking out over the cornfield.

"I must have jarred its head loose when I was tugging on the hat," he rationalized as he unconsciously gripped the hat tighter, feeling it's course texture and surprising dampness. "Must have collected some water after the last rainfall. Well, there's a party with my name on it," he said as he turned around and started heading back the way he had come earlier.

He had only gone about twenty steps when from somewhere close by he heard a load rustling noise as if someone was shuffling their feet in the trampled down cornstalks.

Immediately Mark stopped walking and strained his ears, listening intently to the night, trying to see if he could hear the sound again. After several long drawn out minutes of silence he decided that he must have been hearing things and started walking once more.

The path leading out of the cornfield was clearly marked thanks to Mark's earlier clumsiness. He hurried along the trampled cornstalks and thought he heard the shuffling sound again but this time it was way out in front of him.

"Man, this is starting to really freak me out," he mumbled as he brought the hat up to wipe the sweat from his brow.

As he lowered his arm to his side, the sky was lit up once more, illuminating the cornfield and the path that stretched out in front of him. As the light started to fade and his eyes grew accustomed to the dark, Mark saw standing in the path, maybe forty feet away the silhouette of a large imposing figure.

Raising the arm that held the hat, Mark yelled out and started motioning to the person and that was when he noticed that his hand was completely covered in something dark and sticky. Slowly he brought his hand closer to his face, trying to make out what the dark substance was.

Mark stared at his hand dumbfounded. Completely covering his entire hand was a dark red liquid that remarkably resembled blood. Lowering his hand in disbelief he wondered where the substance could have come from and that's when he noticed that the figure on the path had silently moved a lot closer to him.

"What in the name of... Is there something I can do for you fella," Mark shouted to the man. He tried to remain calm and put up a brave front. When the man didn't answer and didn't seem to be moving. Mark repeated his inquiry only a little louder this time.

Fear rippled up and down Mark's spine. Another flash of lighting pierced the night sky. No longer dark, Mark could clearly see the cornfield and the path he was walking on, the path which was now blocked by the scarecrow Mark had taken the hat from.

Shaking his head in disbelief Mark started to slowly back away from the scarecrow. Fear took control of mark and as he placed his foot down on some unsteady ground, which sent him falling backwards, landing heavily on his backside.

As he sat sprawled out on the crushed cornstalks he heard a dry raspy voice call out, "Give me back what is mine." A moment later, he heard it once more except this time it was much loader and angrier. "GIVE ME BACK WHAT IS MINE!"

Not needing much more encouragement, Mark was back on his feet in record time and looked down at the hat he held clutched in his hand. The fear that Mark had been so gallantly keeping at bay took complete control and he started shaking violently before throwing the hat at the scarecrow. He turned around before it hit the ground and took off running in the opposite direction, never once looking back.

The scarecrow stood motionless in the path for another minute, then two, and suddenly it began to laugh. From behind the scarecrow, two teenage boys emerged laughing hysterically to one another.

"Man that was priceless," they said between fits of laughter.

"That was the best Halloween trick we have ever played. I swear, I think he wet himself. He was so afraid." They continued to joke and laugh together.

"Well I guess he won't be joining our club," they joked further as they bent down to retrieve the hat. "After all he didn't get t..." his voice trailed off as two corn stalk hands encircled the boy's necks from behind. Their laughter was choked into silence as they heard a dry raspy voice say, "I believe that's mine!"

Michael C. Dick *was born in Buffalo, New York and later relocated to Northern Virginia were he currently live with his wife and two children. To read more of Michael's stories please visit it him at his blog at www.michaelcdick.blogspot.com where he encourages feedback from his readers. Michael's stories can also be found in several other horror anthologies and he can be found on Facebook.*

The Life and Loss of Miss Elizibeth Prince
By J. Rodimus Fowler

Miss Prince's family was rich, Kennedy rich or George Bush rich. As you would expect, their summer home was enormous. It was three stories tall everywhere except right in the center. There it was four and a half stories tall with large windows all the way around it. The middle of the top floor was a giant sun room with a beautiful cathedral ceiling.

Her mom used to love to sit there and watch the sunrise and the sunset. She would sit there most evenings having a cocktail or three. Their summer home was in the great state of Tennessee. It was toward the western side, closer to Kentucky than anywhere else. If there were any Hierarchy in the U.S. of A. the Prince's would have been Earls or Dukes or something like that. Her dad was some kind of hot shot scientist, one of the only men in the world who specialized in his particular field.

Elizebeth was too young to understand all of that stuff. Her mom basically followed her dad around from place to place like a loyal puppy. He was frequently sent away to many locations as part of his job, so it wasn't unusual for Miss Elizabeth to be home alone. Well, not alone, she had the staff to keep her company and take care of her.

There was James, who was an elderly gentleman that did all the maintenance and all of the cooking. Then there was Evelyn and her daughter, Susan. Evelyn did the laundry and the cleaning while Susan usually spent her time playing with Miss Elizibeth. Elizibeth liked everybody to call her Miss, it made her feel important. She was only nine years old so everyone thought it was cute. Susan was thirteen and they were both home schooled by Evelyn. Evelyn and James lived in different rooms on the eastern side of the house while the Prince's occupied the rest of the manor.

Mr. and Mrs. Prince were out of town. They were sent to Kentucky where some strange virus was originating. Elizebeth didn't understand, she just knew her parents had left her there with the staff again, which wasn't so bad because she liked to play with Susan. James was cooking dinner and Evelyn was vacuuming the second floor.

Susan and Miss Elizibeth were outside playing hide and seek. Susan was turned around leaning on a car, counting to thirty while Elizibeth was hiding. Miss Elizibeth ducked down in the shrubbery along the eastern side of the large house. Elizibeth heard Susan say, "Ready or not here I come."

Lizzy laid down flat on the ground and slid closer to the bushes. Something stung her on the left hand, quick and painfully. It felt like a bee sting but worse. Elizibeth jumped up from her hiding place and started screaming in pain. Susan ran over, scooped her up and carried her into the house.

Evelyn quickly dropped the vacuum and ran down the steps to see what had happened. James made it there fast as well, leaving his soup slowly cooking on the stove. Upon investigation they saw blood running from Elizibeth's hand and there were two small puncture wounds on her left hand like a snake bite. Evelyn washed and bandaged the wound while James grabbed a shovel from the tool shed and went out to the bushes to find the snake, it may have been venomous. When he arrived at the shrubbery he found the most peculiar of things. The snake was dried up and dead. It looked like one of those snakes you see stuck to the asphalt of the road, dehydrated and lying there for days. That didn't stop the creature from wriggling around though. James chopped its head off with the shovel and put it in a bucket to identify later.

The bite mark on the back of Lizzy's hand already had dark veins streaking away from it like spider webs. They carried Miss Elizibeth to her room where she fell fast asleep. Susan stayed in the room to keep an eye on her. James and Evelyn were downstairs discussing what they should do. They had never seen anything like this.

Susan snuck out to the top of the stairs to over hear what they were saying. Susan leaned in close to hear if they were going to carry Elizibeth to the hospital or call her parents, like they were told to do in case of an emergency. *This was an emergency*, she was thinking to herself. She never even heard Miss Elizibeth Prince walk up behind her, slow and steady, just like she was sleep walking. Miss Elizibeth bent down and took a large bite right out of the side of Susan's neck. The bite was so deep that Susan bled out before Elizibeth could get to her brains. Miss Elizibeth finished eating her best friend's brains and started to walk downstairs, to where the other voices were coming from.

Evelyn walked to one end of the house to call Elizibeth's parents. James turned around and walked back to the kitchen to cut the stove off. This was a serious matter, but there was no need to start a fire because of a stove that was left on. When Miss Elizibeth took the first bite from behind his right knee, he dropped down to the floor in pain. On the way down, he frantically grasped for anything to hold on to and the boiling pot of soup spilled over on top of him. It poured out all over his face; he never even had time to scream before Miss Elizibeth was biting through his skull. The soup gave his brains a different flavor but Elizibeth didn't notice. They were just as good as any other brains to her.

When Evelyn hung up the phone with Elizibeth's father, she ran to the stairs to get to her daughter as fast as she could. When she reached the top of the stairs at the servant's end of the house, she fell down to one knee, she was too late. She heard slow dragging steps coming up the stairs behind her. Then a little girl's hand grabbed her by the leg. She couldn't believe how strong Miss Prince had become. The more she struggled, the farther Miss Elizibeth climbed up her body, pulling on her arms, her hair and her clothes. Finally there was no stopping her and Lizzy bit her on the mouth, pulling her lower lip right off in one delicious bite. Then she kept at it until she got to the brains. Miss Elizibeth ate her fill of flesh and brains then she went and sat in her mom's favorite chair in the upstairs sun room. She slumped over forward and died.

On the drive back to Tennessee, Mr. Prince was trying to explain to his wife that the virus had spread much faster than they had originally thought. He knew the virus couldn't be contained, yet he still wanted to try and save his little girl, he had to. The world was going to end right before his eyes, but he could only think of Miss Elizibeth. When the Prince's made it home, Lizzy's dad stopped in the kitchen to look at the mess that used to be poor James.

Mrs. Prince ran up the center stair case immediately and saw the carnage at the top of the stairs. She started crying uncontrollably and walked right past her chair and her daughter to rest her head on the thick glass window. She stared out at the final sunset she would ever see. Miss Elizibeth Prince's head rose up with a look of pure hunger on her face. She stood up and made her way closer to her mother. She looked up at her mom with the eyes of a hungry child.

As soon as her father reached the top of the stairs, what he saw made him give up right then and there. His little girl was eating his wife's brains and enjoying them thoroughly. Mr. Prince dropped down to his knees and started praying. His mumbled prayers made Miss Elizibeth Prince look over his way. Then she stood up and slowly walked over to her father, dragging her feet as she walked. He saw those eyes that he loved so much, his daughter's eyes, staring right at him. At that exact moment, he wished that he had spent more time with his little girl. She put one of her hands on each of his shoulders as if to say, "*I forgive you Daddy.*" He looked up and smiled widely at her as she bit a hole into the side of his temple. It made the same sound as someone biting into a fresh apple. When she was finished eating she sat back down in her mom's favorite chair and stared out the window. Then her head fell over forward, limp and lifeless, waiting...

Jason 'J. Rodimus' Fowler *was born in Raleigh, North Carolina in the summer of 1976. He writes a variety of dark comedy, horror and suspense with a touch of sci-fi every now and again. He has had a passion for horror and the absurd since he was a small child, which he blames in part on his babysitters, who just happened to have been Monty Python and Rod Serling -via- the Electric God/television. His twisted tales of fear and retribution range from battling hordes of the undead, to true love among demon fodder.*

The Ghost of Gertrude Garvey
By Patrick Shand

Tom, Jake, and Emma stood around the grave of Gertrude Garvey, leaves scuttling around their feet in the soft wind. In the distance, they heard the joyous squeals of the trick-or-treaters, secretly wishing that they too were collecting candy instead of hanging around a graveyard.

"This is giving me goosebumps," Jake said, pulling back his sleeve to show them. "Look. Actual goosebumps. Can we just go?"

"If we leave now, he'll never leave us alone," Emma said. She glanced at the fence, where her big brother, a beefy boy named Boyd, sat sneering with his friends. His gang had caught Emma with Tom and Jake in the street, and her jerk of a brother said that he'd beat them up if they didn't go to the grave and stand over it for ten minutes. Jake tried to make a run for it but, when Boyd grabbed him by the scruff of the neck and threatened to bash his head in, Emma and Tom relented on the condition that Boyd would leave them alone forever.

Boyd nodded slyly, though none of them saw the crossed fingers behind his back.

"D'you think it's true?" Jake asked, staring down at the grave, his voice quavering. "You know... about the ghost?"

"No way," Tom said. "Don't you know anything? Every town has a dumb ghost story. I don't believe that stuff."

Emma nodded, though she was inwardly as frightened as Jake. Everyone knew the story of Gertrude Garvey, the woman who was murdered by her husband on her wedding night. According to legend, Gertrude haunted the graveyard, looking for a person to possess in order to take revenge on men with ill intentions.

"You guys really aren't scared?" Jake asked, his eyes wide and watery.

"Look," Tom said, lowering his voice. "If we stand here, shivering like a bunch of idiots, Boyd is never gonna leave us alone. We gotta show him we're not scared."

Emma stared at the grave, thinking about how it must've felt to be killed by the man you loved on the best night of your life. She wondered why he'd done it.

"How do we show him that?" Jake asked.

Tom smirked, putting his arm around Emma's shoulders. "We dance!" he said. He grabbed her suddenly with both hands, spun her around, and began to do a jig on Gertrude's grave. Emma found herself laughing, all of her worries suddenly gone. She spun around and around, smiling widely. Everything was going to be okay. The two of them were laughing so loudly that it wasn't long before Jake joined in. By the time they collapsed on the grave, sweating and laughing, Boyd and his friends stormed away, defeated.

"Yeah! That's right! That's how we show those jerks," Tom said. "You guys ready to trick or treat?"

"Yeah," Jake said, a big grin on his face.

The three of them got up, walking away from the graveyard with big smiles. Tom was happy that he'd been able to suppress his suffocating fear long enough to make Jake settle down. Jake was happy to be friends with Tom, who he thought was the bravest boy in the world. Emma was happy to take her leave of the grave. She couldn't wait to get home and show Boyd what happens to men with ill intentions. Together, the three of them walked past the gates of the cemetery, the boys completely unaware of how Emma's eyes briefly flashed a menacing red when she looked back at her grace, a wicked grin on her lips.

PATRICK SHAND *is just like Romulus and Remus. Except instead of being raised by ravenous yet friendly wolves, he was raised by books. And also parents. After he read all of the books, comics, and plays ever published (it's true, don't worry), he went on a quest to expand his horizons and write his own material. He has written comics such as Joss Whedon's ANGEL and Spike TV's 1000 WAYS TO DIE, in addition to plays that have been produced in NYC and stories that have been included in anthologies and literary magazines. You can read more about him at* patrickshand.blogspot.com

The Heart Fixer
By Rhiannon Mills

Once upon a dreary Halloween night, when the wind was howling and the rains were pouring and cold, a change in trick-or-treating plans was underway for three sisters in need of adventure and rebellion.

"Where are we going, then?" The youngest sister, Mel, only ten, asked with wide blue eyes and a full sack of sugary treats in her hands.

The oldest sister, Jamie, smirked. "Ya know that house on the hill? The one where the crazy lady lives?"

"We're not supposed to go up there." Mel wrinkled up her nose. "They say she's a witch!"

Kat, the middle sister laughed. "We have to take you trick-or-treating so you have to go where we take you."

"They say she cuts out little kids' hearts!" Mel protested, gripping her bag of candy with clenched fists.

"The story goes that the woman in that old house had her heart broken and that's why, when she has a visitor, she cuts out their hearts. She does it to replace the one she had that was broken so many years ago." Jamie lowered herself to Mel's level to add, "And she also gives out the best candy."

"I wanna keep my heart right where it is!" Mel furiously turned and stalked down the sidewalk in the opposite direction.

"But, Mel, she gives you your heart back. You'll live. Your heart just won't work the same. She uses black magic!" Kat shot after Mel, and grabbed her by her sleeve.

Mel wiped raindrops from her eyes and turned her attention to the old house on the hill. Guarded by two gargoyles on the edge of each side of a rickety gate and a cracked, winding driveway, the house sat back behind a row of trees. It could still be seen above the rest of the town, but sometimes the shadows and fog covered most of it. There were a few busted out windows on the bottom floor. Stray cats surrounded the yards and a bat flew around the chimney, scaring Mel even more than the stone gargoyles.

"She puts a spell on your heart." Kat pushed her hands over her hips, grinning. "I want to see what goes on up there!" Before anyone else could say anything at all, Jamie was running to the top of the hill and had found herself standing between two gargoyles within seconds. "C'mon!"

The other two sisters, both slightly afraid, ran after her in a hurry. Jamie was already fiddling with the gate, looking for a way to open it up. The gate was locked solid and wouldn't budge.

Mel, finding that her sisters were inadequately prepared for their venture, slid between two rails in the gate with absolutely no trouble at all, and laughed at Jamie and Kat. "Duh!" She giggled, then ran up the driveway, suddenly feeling a bit more adventurous.

The two older sisters followed suit, chasing after Mel before she woke the woman up. When they'd reached the top of the driveway, Mel was staring into a broken window, standing on top of a big ugly rock because she was too small to see over the window seals.

Whispering, Mel never took her eyes away from the window. "There's no one in there, Jamie. Completely empty! Cobwebs and furniture covered in sheets. Not even a log in the old broken fireplace."

Jamie brought her eyes up to the window, peering inside to see that Mel was right. The furniture was covered, the fireplace was dilapidated, and everything was dusty and covered in thick cobwebs that were probably abandoned by the spiders that made them long ago. "Then there's nothing to stop us from going in." With that, Jamie pushed the front door open with a few swift movements.

The floor creaked under her feet as she tiptoed inside, her younger sisters both following close behind her.

Kat immediately crossed the distance between the front door and the fireplace and began wiping a thick layer of webs and grime away from a gold framed painting that hung over the fireplace. In the painting a young woman was standing, wearing dark clothes, her dark hair pinned in an ornate bun. Her eyes were fierce and brown, her smirk was haunting, and in her hands she held a small bouquet of wildflowers. "Do you think this is *her*?"

No one answered her question, and the only sound to be heard was a creaking of footsteps following a staircase to the left of the parlor.

Kat frowned. "You coulda' told me you were going upstairs, ya know!" Frustrated, she found the staircase and followed the steps until she found herself at second floor, standing at the edge of a hallway full of doors on either side. "Where you guys at?" Kat walked the hall over creaky boards, hoping that they didn't give way and send her back to the first floor of the old house. "Hello?"

No one answered her.

"Hey, you guys?" Kat called out again.

Still, no answer.

She turned to the first door and wrapped her fingers around the cold brass knob. Before she could twist it open, a pair of cold, unfamiliar hands were on her shoulders, and she could feel a cold, dark presence behind her.

One hand wrapped around her waist, and she could see that one very young and perfectly manicured hand held a blade as she was being pulled backwards.

Her screams carried through the house as she watched the hallway seem to grow longer and longer until she was pulled into a room full of heart shaped pillows and fabrics with heart patterns. Everything was slashed to smitherines, of course, but the hearts were everywhere. Even the dark brass chandelier had black and clear crystals cut into heart shapes.

"Young woman, you know not to come here." A demure young voice whispered into Kat's ear. "I have to fix you!" Then, the woman shoved Kat into an old wooden, high backed chair.

With the sound of swishing, swaying full skirts behind her, Kat knew that the woman had backed away, but she still couldn't move. How would she get out? She couldn't see the door!

"Where are my sisters?" Kat choked on her words, but kept her bravery in check.

"What sisters?" The woman stood in front of her, a sly smirk across her face.

She was exactly as the painting had dictated. Large brown eyes, smirking, dark hair pinned into an ornate design atop her head, but there was a great deal of pain behind her smiles and smirks.

"What did you do with them?" Kat did everything she could to keep herself from crying. "Where did they go?"

"They who?" With that, the woman nearly floated across the floor boards to a dresser and plucked a twisted blade from a silver tray. "This will work! Hold still, will you?" She turned to Kat with a friendly smile, holding the blade out for Kat's inspection.

Kat tried to move from the chair, but couldn't. She was held there by some unknown spell or force.

"This way, you'll never go through what I did. And if you do, it won't hurt you in the way that he, I mean *it*, hurt me." The woman frowned, her eyes saddened.

When she made her way to Kat's side again, she'd shoved the blade into Kat's chest, wiggled it around, and pulled it back out again before Kat could even take one more breath. Blood spurted for a moment, and then drifted into a slow stream.

"Just hold still, okay?" The woman frowned, then dug her hand into the hole she'd made in Kat's chest.

Kat felt her very life draining from the hole.

The woman, witch or whatever she was, pulled Kat's heart out and held it in front of her face. "I just have to fix it! See those veins in there? We have to fix those. That's where all emotion is. We have to cut them so that you can be happy all the time. Just like me!" With that, the crazier-than-Methuselah ghost or whatever she was started cutting away at Kat's heart while Kat was watching.

Blood spurted and fell everywhere, and occasionally, the woman was lick some of it away from her fingers, but within seconds, she'd pushed Kat's heart back into her chest, found a needle and twine, and had her chest sewn back up, lickity split.

"You're all better now, Kat. Can you feel it? No more hurt!"

Kat sat perfectly still. The pain was indescribable. "Where are my sisters?" She managed to mumble under her breath.

The lady sighed. "I think they were allergic to the twine, so I let them go. It's just you and me now, Kat. You have to live here with me."

Kat felt the woman pulling at her chest with more of the twine, finishing the job she'd started, and then everything faded into gray.

Rhiannon Mills *lives deep within the West Virginian mountains where she concocts creepy stories of demons, witches, vampires, and creeps of all creeds. Aside from reading and writing, she enjoys cooking, spending time with her children and her dog, Heidi Mills Demon Pup, and watching historical documentaries that generally no one else likes.*

Equinox
By Geoffery Crescent

"He's so beautiful,"
"Oh...he moves like the wind..."
"I just, I just." And here Sophie burst clean into tears. "I just want a horse so much!"

"It's alright Soph," I said, letting her rest her snotty face on my shoulder. "You know she'll let you ride him later."

"I hate being poor," she muttered viciously. "Daddy won't buy me anything, I hate him."

"Didn't he just buy you a kitten?" I ventured.

"Yes. It's boring." Sophie wiped her rather bulbous nose along her sleeve as the object of our affections rode back round the track. His name was Starshine, and he was fabulous. He was the color of a storm cloud before the rain breaks. He galloped as swift as the wind on the moors, and his hooves were the sound of thunder in the forest. His cargo was an obnoxious brat by the name of Geraldine Posembly-Smythe, but frankly, I didn't care how long she spent moaning about how tiresome her maid was or how many Ferraris she said her father had, the fact was she had a horse and she had said we could ride him. Of course, there had been the long months of promises and cajoling and groveling, and a hideous time when she went back on her word but now, our day had finally come.

I had no doubt that it was all somehow an exercise in improving her reputation amongst the girls in our class. The more people rode her horse, the more would know what a fabulously rich father she had, and what a charming and benevolent young lady was she to let even the poorer and uglier girls ride her beloved Starshine.

I suspected there would be a catch of some sort, perhaps tidying out her locker or worse I feared, doing her geography homework. But I, and especially Sophie were, at present, content to watch her cantering around the yard, safe in the knowledge that we too were soon to be carried on that glistening back, and the giggles when the dowdy riding instructor admonished her paltry riding skills.

Finally, and long after we'd lost interest in Geraldine's endless circling, she slid heavily to the ground and, handing the reigns to her instructor, gave a haughty toss of her head in the direction of the paddock. Following her lead, we seated ourselves on a pile of straw bales, watching as she negligently tossed aside her hat and crop, struggled with her boots for a minute or two, before languidly lying back on the hay, taking no further notice of us.

"Go on," I prompted, exchanging a quick glance with Sophie, who was wearing her customarily bemused expression at the proceedings.

"Go on, what darling?" countered Geraldine, now selecting a choice strand of hay on which to chew.

"Oh don't be such a bore, you know what. What do you want for him?"

"Well now," said Geraldine, sitting back upright with the straw now wedged firmly between her perfect teeth. "I was thinking, perhaps, your souls."

"Oh no!" wailed Sophie. "I already gave mine to Mr. Leeming down at the paper shop for a packet of blackjacks!"

"Don't be stupid Soph!" I said, poking her hard in the ribs with my elbow. "You can't sell your soul. I was thinking more along the lines of…"

"It's souls or nothing girlies, sorry but that's just the way it is," interjected Geraldine, making motions to slide off the hay bale.

"Just a sec," I muttered, ignoring Sophie's continued weeping next to my ear. "Say we do 'sell' you our souls. That means, what, that we have to do whatever you want?"

"Not really." Geraldine slithered off the bale and began pacing slowly in front of us. "I won't expect you to come at my bidding or be held in my thrall or anything silly like that. I just want to own you. I mean, eventually you'll suffer the fires of eternal damnation, but that won't be for another fifty years or so."

I mulled this over in my mind. On the one hand I had absolutely no belief that giving her my soul meant anything to anyone but Geraldine, but surely there had to be some catch? But then the horse truly was beautiful. As I was musing, Starshine himself was led into the paddock, tossing his silvery mane at the indignity of being handled by some stable hand. With a final wrench of his reigns he was free, walking sullenly to a patch of long grass near where we sat.

"Well? Time's ticking on ladies! I'm sure I don't want to miss gangs of poverty stricken trick-or-treaters being turned down by my butler," Geraldine sniggered.

Sophie, who had remained mostly silent throughout our discussions suddenly piped up with, "I'll do it!"

"Good girl!" said Geraldine producing a scrap of paper and a sparkly biro from the pocket of her gullet. "Just sign and date here, and you'll be on your way."

"Not afraid of the fires of eternal damnation then?" I asked, peering over her shoulder as she scrawled.

"I dunno. Just want to ride him." Sophie handed me the paper.

"No thanks, I think I'll watch you go first."

Sophie shoved the paper into Geraldine's awaiting fist, and skipped happily toward Starshine. The sun was just beginning to set; the last rays of light gleaming from his pearlescent coat. He stood patient as Sophie fumbled clumsily with the stirrups, silent as she finally settled into the saddle, gentle as she gave him an overly enthusiastic kick in the ribs. Slowly he gathered speed until he was cantering full pent around the spacious field, now just a wraith in the gathering dusk, vestiges of light catching his mane and Sophie's own long braid. We watched until both were phantoms in the shade, and with a sharp call from Geraldine, Starshine came trotting obediently up to the hay bales. His saddle was empty.

"Where is she?" I cried, turning sharply toward Geraldine.

"I'm sure I don't know my dear," she replied, gathering the reigns as if to head back to the stables. I grabbed her by the front of her shirt, pulling her face close.

"Oh yes you do! Help me find her." I thrust her away, reaching into my trouser pocket for the little torch on my key ring. It was a bright, narrow beam, but as we circled the paddock there was no sign of Sophie. Nor, I realized, any hoof prints.

"There!" pointed Geraldine, sounding neither relieved nor particularly bothered. I followed her arm, and there was Sophie, lying still on the damp turf.

"There's…there's no pulse…"

"Well, she fell off and hit her head silly thing. Should have asked to borrow my hat, but no, she went running off like…"

"She didn't fall." I turned slowly from her dead body. "We would have heard her cry out." An impossible thought struck me. "This is you isn't it? This is you and your 'sell me your soul business?' Isn't it?"

She said nothing.

"Isn't it?" I screamed at her.

"My dear girl," began Geraldine. "Where do you think a horse like that comes from? There isn't a man in the world who could buy me that horse, not even my dear father. Some things in this world must be more..." she paused. "Skillfully obtained."

"What are you going on about?"

"He is mine for a year and a day. Every year and every day, if I can find him the sustenance. Or on my head be it."

"So you're just gonna," I choked, "keep giving him souls? That's monstrous!"

"But darling, when one has everything in the world, one must do what one must to keep oneself entertained. And I just love horses."

"But...what am I suppose to do? I'll tell someone!" I added with sudden vehemence.

"Oh of course. Because everyone will believe a girl who says her friend has a magic horse! Especially one whose father owns, what is it, a Ford Prefect? Don't be ridiculous."

And she walked away then, left me in the middle of dark, damp field, left me clutching a dead body, taking her demon back to his empty stable, whose hooves left no mark on the floor.

Debate rages over who exactly **Geoffery Crescent** *is. Some believe him to be the reincarnation of Phillip Deihl, inventor of the electric ceiling fan. Others think him to be E. F. Summers, a goat farmer from Bavaria. His hobbies include churning butter, melting wax and carving vegetables to look like former US presidents. He is the world expert on soy based meat replacement products. He never completed her Silver Duke of Edinburgh Award and is yet to finish an episode of Deal or No Deal. He has three mothers, but no father, and cannot be killed by conventional means.*

Trick or Cheat
By Rebecca Snow

"I don't think Jim's coming," Sally said. She picked at a stray pink feather on her boa.

Ted shrugged and used the toe of his shiny cowboy boots to kick a clod of rust-colored dirt across the crumbing sidewalk. A scowling pumpkin flickered from a distant porch.

"He said he would, but it's already 10:15. All the good stuff will be gone if we don't go soon."

The full moon stared down at the children as they paced the small patch of uneven cement like they were picketing for equal pay. Leaves floated from the trees and landed in a silent blanket across the pavement. A small car clattered past, letting out a wheezing cough as it turned the corner.

"What was that?" Sally asked. Her eyes darted to a shadowy patch of brush just beyond the closed iron gate.

"Probably a cat," Ted said, kicking the six-foot fence.

He wrapped his fingers around the bars and strained to test their strength. Nothing but his wiry frame shook. Branches rustled near his exposed digits. Releasing the bars as if they'd burnt holes in his skin, he stepped back onto the sidewalk. A moan rose from the thicket. As the two children stared, the quivering shrubbery vomited a rotting cadaver.

"Great job, moron," Sally said. "Now how are we going to make it to the porch?"

Ted hopped from side to side and watched the zombie rock with his movement.

"I'll lure him away." Ted picked up a long stick and poked it through the bars at the creature. "You make a break for it."

Sally dropped her flowered pillowcase in the gutter and gaped at the boy.

"You want me to go inside by myself and grab the goods?" She crossed her arms over her sock-stuffed corset and raised a sharp-penciled brow. "In these heels?" Her left ankle wobbled in support.

"Take the shoes off. It's not like you'll put a run in your fishnets."

He tempted the monster by picking at a scabbed over mosquito bite. The corpse took a few stumbling steps away from the latched gate and licked the air with its blackened tongue.

"See, he'll follow me anywhere," Ted said as he skipped a few steps more. "You'll be fine."

"What about Jim?" Sally asked.

"If he wants any of our haul, he'll have to fight me for it." Ted palmed his fist and cracked his knuckles.

"Our haul?" Sally stomped her foot. "I won't go by myself. There's no way I can carry enough for the both of us."

Ted faked left. The maggot-ridden pile of flesh threw its sinewy arms into the fence that blocked it from its prey.

"I think you might be onto something." He tapped his pinched lips with a thumbnail. "I've got it," he said with a finger snap. "I'll lead him around the back of the fence. You head to the porch. I'll run back around and meet you there."

"Promise?" Sally said in a hoarse whisper.

Ted nodded. "Cross my heart."

Sally toed off her stilettos. Flashing her a snaggle-toothed, sideways grin, Ted winked and ran around the iron-barred corner. The rotten man dragged after the sprinting boy, leaving the gate unattended. Sally snatched her candy sack and ran to the gate. The heavy latch squealed as she raised it. With a shrieking scream, the heavy gate swung on its hinges. Hurrying through the widening space, the girl managed to bring the door to a slow halt and reverse its progress. The rusted closure clanked as it met the iron catch. Sally spun and ran on tiptoes up the packed dirt path. Her pillowcase flailed from her clinched fingers.

As she reached the wooden stair rail, Sally bent at the waist and huffed to catch her breath. A grinning jack-o-lantern winked up at her as it guarded a trashcan brimming with of unopened bags of snack-sized candy. Her eyes bulged and her jaw went slack as she took a few halting steps toward the treasure-filled container. She dropped her cotton pillow cover and began to shove bags of Reece's Cups and Snickers into the opening.

Movement in the tree-strewn yard caught her eye. Several figures pulled themselves toward the gingerbread trimmed Victorian. Sally squeaked as they cut off her escape from the yard. Grabbing her hall, she turned and fled up the sagging plank stairs. Her bag snagged on a crooked nail. A golf ball-sized gap tore in the side and spilled a trail of Midgees and Starburst mints as she traversed the wraparound porch.

She turned the corner and stepped into empty space. One knee collided with the floorboards while her foot dropped into the porch's crawlspace through a gap in the planks. Something dug into her thigh, ripping stitches loose in her stockings.

"Ted!" she shrieked and scrambled to pull her foot from the open space.

She rubbed the snapped elastic strings. The skin underneath was broken. A large splinter jutted from the wound looking as though a cartoon rocket had crash-landed on the moon. Pain erupted from the puncture as she ripped the wooden shard free. The zombies stumbled and fell as they made their way up to the porch. Careful of the yawning breach, Sally dragged herself and her bag of cavities across the warped flooring.

She rose to her feet and limped to the backside of the house. Three rickety boards led down to the darkened yard. She gripped the wobbling railing and hopped down the steps. A gumball squeezed from the hole in her bag and clattered along down beside her. Sticking in the shadows, she made her way around the house. The corpses were tangled into a groaning pile of festering limbs. One of the shamblers must have dropped into the hole and blocked the way.

When she reached the front path, she looked back at the house. Ted had disappeared. The gate loomed ahead of her. She pulled up the squeaky latch and edged through the opening, careful not to let go of the heavy bars. Slamming the catch home, she took three floundering steps and collapsed on the curb to inspect the oozing hole in her leg.

"I knew you could do it," Ted said, unfolding himself from beneath a large oak tree growing outside the iron bars.

Jim rose from the shadows and shoved his hands in his pants pockets. A black cape drooped over his slumped shoulders.

Ted stretched his arms above his head and yawned. "That zombie I had following me got tangled in some brush at the corner of the yard." He pointed to where the fence followed the sidewalk down a side street. "Jim was here when I got back."

Sally stood, her eyes disappearing into angry slits. A scowl crumpled her smooth forehead. Ted rubbed his hands together like a mad scientist. Jim ducked back to the safety of the sheltering oak.

"What'd you bring us?" he asked. His eyes twinkled in the moonlight, his badge flashed in the lights of a passing car.

"Where were you?" Sally shrieked. "You promised you'd meet me on the porch. Those things attacked me. Look at my leg." She pressed her palms on either side of her torn flesh and watched as a fresh blossom of blood bloomed from the deep gouge. "I'm bleeding."

"It's only a scratch." The boy leaned around the girl to catch a glimpse of her bulging sack resting on the rocky cement. "What did you get?"

Pushing the bangle bracelets up her arms as if they were sleeves, Sally stepped toward him. Ted took a backwards step into the fence. Sally lifted a clenched fist and took another limping stride. The boy leaned against the iron barrier, one arm reached through and fumbled in the shrubbery. When the girl was within striking distance, Ted screamed and yanked his arm from the bars. Jagged edges of torn flesh circled his wrist.

"That thing bit me," Ted shouted, gripping his wrist to staunch the blood. He dropped to the ground and writhed in agony.

"I'll bet you bit yourself," Sally said.

Her fists unclenched as she returned to her cotton pillowcase. She hefted it over her shoulder and shuffled down the street.

"Where do you think you're going?" Jim asked. His eyebrows rose in questioning arcs.

"Home," Sally said. "I've had enough tricks for one night."

Ted's howls followed her as she passed the grinning pumpkins that leered from porch railings. When the shouting ceased, she glanced over her shoulder. Jim stood over Ted's twitching form. She turned a corner, and the shouting resumed. The pitch was different, but Sally was sure Ted was only yelling louder so she'd hear.

"Faker," she mumbled as she wound her way home though the crisp autumn air.

Rebecca Snow lives in Virginia with her husband and clan of cats. Her short fiction has been published in a number of small press anthologies. Find her online at cemeteryflower.blog.com or follow her on Twitter @cemeteryflower

Bets Beware
By L.J. Landstrom

"Dude, pull over, that's the one!" shouted Ryan from the backseat.

Following his friend's order, Trevor slowed the minivan to a stop and peered down the long gravel driveway that dead-ended at a dimly lit shack in the woods. "I don't know, this looks pretty damned Wrong Turn."

Trevor's girlfriend leaned over from the passenger side and grabbed his hand. "Oh come on, it'll be fun, Trev! You aren't afraid, are you?"

Ryan and his date laughed from the backseat, prompting Trevor to turn around and slug his friend in the arm.

"No! I just don't know if we have enough time. I told my mom I'd pick up my little sister from her trick-or-treating party at 10:00, and if I'm late, I'm busted."

"Whatever, we had a bet, dude. You go trick-or-treating at whichever house I choose and I give you twenty bucks."

"Yeah, but you didn't say we were going to be driving out to the friggin' Appalachian mountains to hillbilly central! I've seen this movie, man—the one where the teenagers drive out to the middle of nowhere on Halloween night to pull some stunt and end up hanging on meat hooks in the back of some sicko's cabin! Twenty ain't gonna cut it!"

"You're not pulling a stunt though, just a little innocent trick-or-treating. Tell you what, I'll make it fifty," said Ryan, "but you have to actually say 'trick-or-treat, I'm a pretty princess' when they open the door, no matter what."

Trevor glanced over at his smiling girlfriend and knew it was time to man-up.

Exiting the minivan, Trevor grabbed the final touch to his parasitic twin costume—the protruding fetus' miniature top hat—and began walking down the driveway. The other three followed closely behind. "I can't believe I'm doing this. What do you think they're gonna be like in there?"

Ryan laughed, "Well, out here it's all in the family, if you know what I mean! I hear the outcome is sort of a Neanderthal-type human."

"Great."

Trevor proceeded toward the door, the others stopping just short of the cabin in order to duck behind some brambles to watch. Trevor tripped and fell into something squishy. "Sick!" he exclaimed, hastily pulling himself to his feet.

The girls backed away from the rotting mash of flesh. "Gross, you totally have dead animal guts all over your shirt!"

"Sh, he's at the door."

Trevor stood on the collapsing porch and cautiously looked at his surroundings. It was dark, very dark, the only light coming from the moon and one room of the tiny shack. There was a potent smell to his left, a combination of vinegar and strong body odor; it burned his nostrils. Looking down, he noticed a chicken carcass at his feet, alive with hungry maggots. He cranked his head to see if he could catch a glimpse of anything through the crack in the curtains but saw nothing He raised his fist to knock on the door, but then jumped back when a voice from the darkness startled him.

"*Hellooo, my precious,*" it hissed.

Giggles followed.

"Damn it, Ryan, not cool!" Trevor whisper-shouted into the brambles.

"Then put on your big boy panties and get this thing done," returned Ryan.

Trevor wiped the sweat from his hands, straightened his twin and knocked.

And waited.

He could hear movement through the house, not footsteps, but a sort of thumping and sliding. "Just a minute," called a sweet, feminine voice from inside. Trevor felt instant relief; first, it was a woman, and secondly, she didn't sound inbred at all.

Trevor's heart slowed and a few moments later he heard the unlatching of multiple locks. The knob turned and the door pulled open.

In the entryway stood a torso. A female torso.

Trevor dropped his plastic pumpkin, spilling candy across the floor.

"Oh ya poor thing," said the torso-woman, "you've gone and dumped your candies." She reached to the floor with one arm, the knuckles of her other fist resting on the floor for balance. As she gathered up the candy, the moonlight illuminated her face, half of which dripped down like the wax of a lit lop-sided candle.

"I...I..." stammered Trevor. "Tri...tri...treat."

"Well I'll be, sweetie, you're one of those slow boys, ain't ya? What a scary costume you done got yerself there. What is ya, a two-headed beast? Look, I's gonna find you something real special for your goodie bag. You just wait here whiles I fetch somethin'."

Torso-woman placed both knuckles on the floor and began to propel herself around the shack by her arms, like an orangutan. Trevor felt something warm running down his legs, which he hopelessly willed to move.

She rummaged through boxes and cupboards, frantically knuckle-crutch pacing around while looking for something. Trevor's mind was flooded with all the vile possibilities.

"Now you listen here, boy," she called, "I know you must be wundrin' 'bout me, but don't you worry none. I ain't one of those crazies you find out here in these parts. I done lost my legs in a motorcicle accident last year. Durned near killed me. And I know my face ain't pretty no more, but I can't afford no fancy plastic surgery."

She honed in on a black garbage bag and half crawled in to excavate. Her honeyed voice and explanation of her appearance eased his paralysis somewhat, and he managed to pick up his pumpkin.

"I...I'm sorry to bother you," he forced out. "I'll just—"

"Ahhhhhhhhhhhh!" Torso woman screamed from inside the bag. "Don't you go nowhere, boy!"

Trevor froze again. He felt the panic rising from his feet up to his head, which now pulsed with the rapid beat of his heart. He clenched his pumpkin tightly and held his breath.

"I's got a surpriiiiiise for you, young'in."

Holding the 'surprise' behind her torso with one hand, she shimmied her way sideways toward the door, rocking from side to side, the way one would move a heavy dresser by themselves. She grinned with great satisfaction, revealing a toothless mouth.

She dropped the item in his pumpkin. He didn't dare look down.

"Th...thanks," he said, and much to his surprise, he was able to high-tail it out of there.

"Happy Halloween!" he heard as he bee-lined for the minivan.

Ryan and the girlfriends jumped him from the brambles, laughing hysterically.

"Dude, what the hell was that?" Ryan laughed. "Was she hot or what?"

"Shut up! Let's just go!"

The foursome walked hastily to the minivan and jumped in. Trevor took his place in the driver's seat and engaged the power locks. He placed his parasitic twin over his lap in hopes of hiding his wet pants.

"You guys smell piss?" asked Ryan from the backseat.

"No."

Trevor did a three-point turnaround and peeled out and onto the road, shooting loose gravel all around them.

"Dang, take it easy, buddy!"

Trevor's girlfriend tried to take his hand and lean onto his shoulder but he denied her. Rejected, she looked into his pumpkin for some chocolate comfort. "Hey, who gave you this cute music box?"

Trevor had forgotten to look at his 'special' surprise. "*She* did."

"Cool!" She wound it up and the familiar tune of Old MacDonald began to play.

"Hey Ryan, where's my fifty bucks?" Trevor called out.

"You didn't say 'trick-or-treat, I'm a pretty princess.' No deal!"

Trevor, now doing 50 mph on the dark, windy country road, reached back to rough up Ryan in earnest. The car swerved, catching the shoulder and nearly forcing them off the road. "Jerk!"

The car fell silent. Trevor was furious and humiliated; who knew if his girlfriend could even respect him after that pathetic display. He wished he had never taken the bet. And how ridiculous…paralyzed by the site of a torso-chick. He could have punted her like his last winning kick at homecoming. He would never live this one down.

He reached for the stereo and cranked it up. The pulsing base of techno shook the car. He pushed the gas pedal to the floor. He knew the aggressive driving scared the others, but he also knew they had the sense not to say anything about it.

Music blaring, several more miles distanced between them and Torso-Woman, Trevor felt his pulse finally beginning to slow. The silence from his friends was beginning to feel awkward. "Hey Ryan, you got my fifty out yet?" he called to the backseat.

No response.

He turned down the radio.

"Ryan?"

Trevor glanced in his rearview mirror to get a look at his passengers. Two hideously disfigured eyes stared back at him—dark, drooping, bloodshot eyes. It was a torso-*man*.

"Trick," it snarled, grinning from deformed ear to deformed ear. "*I'm* a pretty princess!"

Trevor and his girlfriend whipped around in a panic, catching a glimpse of Ryan and his date as the torso-man's oversized hands tightened around each of their throats, drawing them closer so he could gnaw at their flesh.

"E-I-E-I-O," he sang.

L.J. Landstrom *lives in the rainy state of Washington. In her spare time she enjoys ghost hunting and writing.*

The Damned
By Shawn M. Riddle

"There is nothing we can do for her. We have to get out of here, right now," Charles said as the front door buckled in its frame, the old wood beginning to splinter. Tim looked down at his beloved Clara and began to sob. Tears welling in his eyes, he turned away from her and followed Charles down the hall toward the stairway. "We've got to find a way to get to the roof, that's our only chance," said Charles, panting heavily and taking the stairs three at a time.

The two men reached the top level of the old house just as the front door buckled and the creatures began swarming into the house. The high pitched shrieks of the beasts pierced their ears and made their blood run cold. They didn't know where these things came from or even what they were, but the chaos that followed in their wake was unmistakable. Every human that succumbed to their power became one of their minions, mindless and savage.

It had been only a few hours since the 'invasion' began and it seemed as if most of the human population was now under their power. Everyone who was not affected was being killed in the most brutal manner possible. Torn limb from limb, the remains of their bodies left everywhere. These demons seemed fixed on a single purpose, the extermination of all humans.

Charles, Tim, and Clara had barricaded themselves in one of the houses on the street, hoping that if they stayed quiet and out of the way that they would be overlooked. To their sorrow, that was not the case. Clara had begun to change and had fallen unconscious. Her beautiful eyes still wide open as she slept, their brilliant blue replaced by the black of madness. As she had awoken, she attacked the two men and Charles had been forced to kill her. He crushed her skull with the broken leg from a large table.

Now the 'demons' and their human slaves were in the house, searching for more prey. Tim and Charles ran down the upstairs hall until they found the pull string to the attic staircase. Hearing the creatures chasing behind them they had no choice but to ascend to the attic in an attempt to escape.

They climbed the ladder and pulled the staircase up just as the mixed horde of creatures spotted them and began to run down the hall in their direction. The small demons screeched in rage at the loss of their prey, their human slaves joining the cacophony.

Sweating profusely and shaking, Tim and Charles looked at one another, then to the staircase they had just pulled up. "That's not gonna keep them for long, now what the hell are we supposed to do?" Tim said.

"I didn't see you coming up with any brilliant plans, we made it this far didn't we?" Charles said.

"Made it this far? What the hell are you talking about? We made it to a damn attic! I wouldn't call this very far," Tim said as he punched Charles in the face with all he could muster. "That's for Clara you son of a…" A huge crash below them interrupted Tim's fury. The creatures were beginning to break through the attic hatch.

Charles wiped the blood from his lip as he stood. "We don't have time for this." He looked around the attic, noticing some light at the far end. "This way." He motioned for Tim to follow. The two men made their way across the attic, straight to a vented window at the far side.

Tim pushed on the window, but it stayed firm in its frame. He yelled and screamed as he kicked at the frame, the solid wood of the louvers not budging.

"Move over man," Charles said as he smashed at the window with the leg of the table he had used only moments earlier to kill Clara. The louvers cracked with each blow and finally gave way and splintered. "Come on," Charles yelled as he squeezed his body through the small opening onto the roof. Tim followed right behind, the shrieks of the creatures still echoing downstairs as they tried to break through.

As they ran across the roof to the side of the house, one of the demons jumped onto the roof and began to shriek, the high pitched noise of its wails resonating for what must have been miles. Tim stopped dead in his tracks his eyes opened wide and his mouth gaped, he fell to the roof on his hands and knees. Charles used the club and struck a blow to the creatures head, sending it careening off the roof onto the ground below. He turned to Tim and grabbed him by the arm. "Hurry up man, we have to…" his sentence stopped in mid word as he saw his friends eyes begin to glaze over black, a feral look of lunacy spread over Tim's face as he stood.

Tim, now one of the demon's minions, shrieked the high pitched shriek of the damned and lunged. Charles managed to side step his former friends attack and tripped him, sending Tim falling face first to the roof. Tim snarled and jumped to his feet, saliva dripping from the corners of his mouth, and those blank, black, dead eyes bore into Charles. He lifted his club over his head and brought it crashing down onto Tim's skull. The brittle bones of the skull shattered on impact and Tim fell back down. His body rolled off the side of the roof and to the ground.

Charles fought back the urge to scream, in the last few minutes he had killed his best friend and his wife. In the last hour he had seen more death than most seasoned combat soldiers. But he was going to live, someone had to live, to survive.

He ran across the roof and jumped to the roof of the house next door. The creatures now hot on his trail. He jumped down to the garage roof and to the ground where he turned and ran up the street. Dozens of demons and human minions were now following him, shrieking for his blood. He turned the corner onto Knight Road and ran toward the church at the far end, hoping beyond hope that he could reach the church and maybe he could take refuge there.

He was only a few hundred feet from the church when the front doors burst open and more creatures came pouring out of the entrance. He stopped in his tracks, unable to move forward or go back. The demons and their minions surrounded him on every side. He brandished his club in both hands and swung it at the creatures as they approached. One of the demons moved forward and faced Charles. Its needle sharp teeth dripping with blood and saliva, its black eyes bore into his.

"What are you waiting for?" Charles screamed as he continued to swing his club. The horde of creatures just stood, staring at him, the night became deathly silent. The demon in front took a step toward him, Charles lifted his club to strike but stopped before he swung, unable to move. The demon let out a piercing shriek. It pierced Charles ears and felt like a knife in his brain. He couldn't concentrate, his thoughts were disjointed, almost as if they were being wiped away like chalk from a chalkboard. He dropped his club, he heard a voice in his mind that he could not ignore or resist. "You're mine now human, now join my brood in the hunt, we shall rid the world of this human blight and reclaim it for our own."

Charles's eyes turned from brown to a glossy black, the man he once was was no more, he followed his new brethren into the night, in search of prey.

Shawn M. Riddle *is from the Northern Virginia area, just outside Washington D.C. He currently works as a construction Quality Assurance Engineer. He grew up on a steady diet of George A. Romero and slasher movies. He is also currently working on his first novel in the Zombie genre. He runs a fan group for author David Moody on Facebook and can be found there as Shawn 'Rotting Corpse' Riddle.*

In A Cat's Eye
By Louise Herring-Jones

"Are you sure you want this one?" Dad interrupted Ginny's study of the large pumpkin. "Isn't it too long?"

"Dad, it's just right," Ginny answered.

"Whatever you say." Dad paid the farmer.

* * *

At home, Ginny's brother Arnie stared at the oddly shaped pumpkin resting on newspapers atop the kitchen table. "Aren't you entering the school's jack-o-lantern contest? How can you win with this? It looks more like a watermelon than a pumpkin!"

"It's going to be great. My name will be in the newspaper as the winner," Ginny said.

Arnie walked away, shaking his head.

Ginny carved an angled opening around the pumpkin's stem so the lid would not fall inside. Pulling on the stem, she stretched out the fibers that clung underneath. The pumpkin's insides smelled like yesterday's garbage. Holding her breath, she hacked at the fibers.

The pumpkin flesh resisted her efforts. Twice, the seedy mass seemed to pull back as she yanked at thicker tendrils.

It's late. I'm tired. It will all seem silly in the morning.

* * *

Mom called, "Breakfast in the dining room; only pumpkins allowed on the kitchen table. One or two pancakes, Ginny?"

After breakfast, Arnie left for soccer practice. Dad and Mom drove him and went grocery shopping. Ginny stayed home to carve her jack-o-lantern. Selecting the flattest end, she drew eyes, a nose and a mouth. When a scary face grimaced back, Ginny began carving. As she worked, she found a few stray strands and seeds. But each time she reached inside, she felt a tug, just as she had the night before. She gazed at the clock, wondering what was taking her parents so long.

After many careful cuts, the face had narrow eyes with vertical, elongated pupils, a triangle nose, and a Cheshire cat's smile right out of *Alice in Wonderland*. Ginny carried the pumpkin out the back door. Setting it down on the concrete patio, Ginny spread more newspaper and shook a spray paint can. She wondered if she should start painting with both her parents gone.

I'm almost thirteen. I can do this alone. Ginny moved the pumpkin onto newspaper, picked the lid off, and placed it beside the pumpkin. Taking one last look inside, Ginny spied a seed and reached into the hollowed globe.

A strong tug made Ginny fall to her knees. She strained against the pumpkin's force, pulled out her hand, and scuttled away to think from a safe place. There was no one else to test whether what Ginny felt was real or "only her imagination." As she stared at the half-completed jack-o-lantern, she thought about starting over with a new pumpkin that didn't yank back. *But, the contest deadline is Monday. I don't know when Dad and Mom will be back. I just won't put my hand inside again.*

Having made her decision, Ginny stood up, collected the paint can and spray-painted the pumpkin a glossy black. As the paint dried, she made feet for the pumpkin-cat from art clay. She sprayed the four paws black, also. While the clay feet dried, she picked eight long straws from a broom. She cut four small holes on either side of the nose for the whiskery straws, moved the paws into place, and replaced the lid. An angry black pumpkin-cat glared at her as she cleaned the patio. Picking up her supplies, Ginny left the pumpkin outside to finish drying and went inside to watch cartoons.

* * *

Just before lunchtime, Arnie walked through the back door with an armful of grocery sacks. "Here squirt," he said. "Help." Ginny bolted out the door and saw Dad leaning over the pumpkin.

"Great job." He kneeled over the black pumpkin-cat. "But I think you missed a spot."

Ginny cried, "No," too late. As he pulled open the lid and reached in, Dad's hand and arm, followed by his whole body, flowed into the opening with a loud "whoosh." Fighting back tears, Ginny dived into the pumpkin with her hands held together.

"Whoosh!"

Faint from the smell of rotting slime and paint fumes, Ginny landed with a thump in a long tunnel draped with orange strands. She pulled herself up, but slipped on the slick carpet of seeds. She stood more slowly the second time. As she walked, calling "Dad" over and over again, the slimy strings slapped her face and arms. She pushed through the dangling fibers and yelled, "Dad, wait, please wait."

After what seemed like hours of struggle against the pumpkin, Ginny plopped down on the orange mess, buried her face in her hands, and cried.

"Ginny, it's okay; I'm here." She felt Dad's comforting hand on her shoulder. "Don't worry, I won't leave you again." Dad helped Ginny stand.

Ginny hugged her Dad and buried her wet face in his plaid flannel shirt. "Can we go home now, Daddy?" she asked, turning her face up to her father.

""Yes, let's get out of here!" he said, pulling out a pocket knife. "How about some real pumpkin carving?"

"Cut away, Dad." Ginny watched as her father hacked through the wall.

Together, they stepped into a sunlit field. Pumpkins lay in rows just beyond the edge of the mown grass. It was the same patch where they had bought the mysterious pumpkin. Dad dialed Mom on his cell phone. She picked them up in the station wagon.

"That's the most ridiculous story I've ever heard," Mom said after Ginny and Dad told her about their adventure. "And you didn't need to walk over here to buy a new pumpkin. There's nothing weird about the jack-o-lantern Ginny already carved. I was just looking at it when you called. It's a fine job, maybe good enough to win the contest."

"I don't know about that, "Ginny said. "I don't ever want to go near it again." Dad nodded his head in agreement.

"Well, you don't have to worry about that. You won't even have to light it," Mom said.

"I'll have to put a light in it if I enter the contest."

"No, you won't." Mom laughed. "When I left, Arnie said he was going to light it for you. It should already be on the front porch when we get home."

103

"Oh, no," Ginny and Dad said together as Mom turned into the driveway. The black cat jack-o-lantern sat on the porch, but there was no light burning inside. They all searched, but could not find Arnie.

"Here we go again," Dad said. "How about picking me up at the pumpkin patch?" Dad opened the lid and disappeared into the jack-o-lantern.

"Mom, let's go," Ginny said.

"In there?" Mom asked, pointing at the malevolent pumpkin-cat that had just swallowed Dad.

"No, back to the pumpkin patch. Don't worry, it's probably just your imagination."

Ginny laughed as she led Mom to the station wagon. "What a jack-o-lantern! My name will be in the newspaper this time, for sure."

Louise Herring-Jones *writes mainstream, historical, and speculative fiction as well as non-fiction. Three of her science fiction stories are included in anthologies. Her historic baseball article "A Georgia Yankee: The Legend of Johnny Mize" appeared in the <u>2010 Maple Street Press Yankees Annual</u>. She is a veteran reporter for The Daily Dragon Online. She practices law in Alabama and frequently represents children. Visit her website at <u>http://www.louiseherring-jones.com</u>.*

The Full Moon
By Stuart Conover

Harry and Patty had time to kill while their parents were busy picking out pumpkins to carve and drinking a spiced cider that none of the kids weren't allowed to have. All of the kids were given free range on the farm for the afternoon and early night. They were having a blast! It was a yearly tradition for the kids to keep themselves occupied and back into the beds in their cabins by ten while the adults would party late into the night. Between a spooky old house, a haunted forest planned for the night, two different corn mazes, learning to pumpkin carve, and hayrides, there was tons of things to do! All of the cabins were also fully loaded with televisions, books, and all kinds of activities for the kids who can't easily sleep to keep having fun but usually most were ready to pass out pretty early.

It was a celebration that the same group performed each year on the night of the full moon closest to Halloween. They were a giant family that would get together and celebrate the season in all of its glory.

Unfortunately for Harry, who had to take care of his sister, Patty didn't want to do anything but crafts. He had to work to talk her into going on the hayride when it started to get dark and who wanted to go on a hayride?

The full moon was slowly rising into a cloudless sky and day turned to night, he shuffled behind his sister slowly walking toward the hayride that it looked like only they would be on.

"This is dumb," he muttered.

"Well it was your idea and it sounds like fun so let's hurry up already!" Patty sniped at him.

The tractor that would be taking them seemed to be a patchwork of rusted pieces of metal slapped together and sounded like it could barely run. The trailer they were supposed to climb into seemed to barely be held together by the nails that were driven through the boards. The hay barely seemed to cover the bottom and actually seemed to be falling out through it in parts. When they looked up at their driver he was shrouded in the shadows of his straw hat wearing overalls that seemed to be falling apart.

"Get along kiddies," he rasped, "It's going to be dark soon and we want to be well on our way before the wolves wake up."

He laughed as they slowly got into the back of the trailer.

"He didn't mean real wolves did he, Hare?" Patty asked with a hint of concern to her voice.

"Of course not, he's just trying to scare us and it seems you are just gullible enough to believe him. We're on a fake farm, it's nothing to worry about," sighed Harry. "I swear you'd believe anything."

Right as they were settled in, both children jumped from a grinding thunderous noise that filled the air as the tractor's engine turned on and dark smoke billowed up, blackening the already darkening sky.

"All Aboard!" rattled off the madman as he cackled with glee. "This night's full moon will surely give you something interesting to see!"

The tractor started taking the two children on the final ride of the night before all of the kids had to be back in bed. It seemed so unfair to Harry who had just turned fifteen. One year away from when he would be considered an adult just made him feel stuck. Sure in the eyes of school and most of society he would still be considered a teenager, barely able to drive, but his extended family saw things slightly differently.

The tractor ride was the last thing they'd be able to do tonight with it getting late and Harry wanted to curse his sister for getting him on such a lame event. But what can you do? The darkness was coming up quickly and the full moon in the sky was casting shadows that covered the trailer and seemed to move with the wind. As they passed one of the returning tractors they noticed that back appeared empty and none of the children that had gone out seemed to be returning.

"Here's where they used to bury the dead," their driver suddenly barked as they passed through what appeared to be a small graveyard. "The ghosts of the children who didn't make it through the nights can still be heard crying here in the dead of night!"

"Harry I want to go back," his sister said with her hand tightening around his. Harry just looked at his sister with such a clear look of disgust that she just looked away.

As they cleared the graveyard and entered the forest they could see lights moving in the trees, what looked to be little fires moving.

The driver looked at them nervously and seemed to speed the tractor up.

"It's getting late kids we should head back."

The rest of the ride went by in a blur and they weren't told much more about the area. Right as they were closing in on the area where they had passed the first tractor, they heard a howl in the distance. Their driver swore and sat up straight looking frantically back and forth. As they cleared a corner he laughed and pointed.

"It's just a dog, children. It looks as if the wolves aren't out quite yet and you'll be home safe and sound in just a few minutes."

Patty finally let go of her brother's hand, but still looked like she didn't want anything to do with him after the look he'd given her. As they pulled back into the yard, Patty jumped out and ran toward their cabin.

"You're always so mean to me!" she yelled over her shoulder.

Harry sighed and started to follow her. It was almost time for the curfew and he had to make sure she was in bed before it was getting late and had to make sure he was inside as well. As he was walking toward his cabin, a cool breeze filled the air as he realized exactly how quiet it was.

There was absolutely no one around.

As he walked up to the cabin, the bushes started to rustle. The full moon illuminated everything, but there were shadows between him and the door and the bushes were still rustling.

He slowly walked toward the entrance, eyes not able to leave the bushes. He passed them and right as he was reaching for the doorknob he heard a branch crack behind him. He looked back right as something was jumping right at him!

"The doors locked and I forgot my keys!"

"Patty, Christ, you shouldn't have run ahead. I'll let you in."

He unlocked the door and told her to go straight to bed. He planned on making a quick stop at a vending machine by the main lounge to grab a bag of chips and a cola before it was time to turn in. Then put on some horror films before he passed out.

He hurried toward the lounge. He had to be back in the cabin quick or he'd be in a lot of trouble if anyone noticed that he was out. A year away from being an adult and still having to follow a curfew was stupid, but he didn't want to get in trouble. He raced toward the vending machine and was stocking up on snacks when he heard the parent's party apparently in full swing.

They had some kind of an African drum sounding beat going on and everyone seemed to be cheering. He couldn't help but wonder what they were up to in there and what kind of a game they were playing. As much as he wanted to go back to the cabin he couldn't help but inch toward the banquet room all of the parents were in. The windows were blacked out from the inside so if he was going to actually look in, he would have to sneak a door open.

He should go back. All he could do was quietly walk down the hall.

He had to go back. The drums were getting louder and the light flickered along the frame.

He needed to go back. Instead he cracked open the door.

He didn't want to grow up now. He couldn't move, transfixed before him. His parents were there. Everyone's parents were there, but there was nothing human in the room. The drums played on but nothing human danced to them. It was only creatures, howling, shrieking, and fur covering their skins.

Suddenly, everything made sense and Harry didn't want to grow up. He didn't want to become one of them. He didn't want to fit in. He didn't want to be a monster, a werewolf.

Stuart Conover *is a horror author that lives in the Chicagoland area. He is also the founder of iScream Productions, and editor of Buy Zombie. A true horror fanatic he goes out of his way to find the latest in everything zombie related. When not delving into the land of horror he spends his days working in IT and his nights full of terror with his wife Leah and his chocolate lab Ali.*

Check Your Candy
By Eloise J. Knapp

It turned out thirteen was the age I could trick-or-treat alone with just my friends. No chaperones. No limit on how many neighborhoods we hit. No taking my six year old twin brothers.

The constant fights with my parents paid off. Two years running starting in early September I harassed them about letting this year be *The Year*. The year I could go solo. Two days before Halloween my mom caved, giving me only two rules. "Go anywhere you want, just not 4th street. Be home by 9:30pm and that's final."

9:30pm was way too early, but I didn't want to push my luck. As for the 4th street thing...I knew why mom didn't want me over there and it was *so* stupid. Plus, that part of the neighborhood was a lot nicer than she remembered it being! There were even a few bigger, nicer houses. Some of them would definitely have full sized candy.

If my friends—Jenny-O, M.M., and Dawson—wanted to go over there, I'd say yes. No chaperones, remember? But a part of me didn't want to *totally* go against what mom said. So unless they really pushed me, I wouldn't.

Jenny-O, Dawson, and I sat on the back porch of my house waiting for M.M. Our house was shutdown, closed to trick-or-treaters since mom and dad had to take the twins out this year. And, of course, since the folks were out, we could kick it in peace.

"It's about time you grew up," Dawson said as he passed me the 2-liter of Coke. "If you couldn't go alone this year, I'd officially dub you lame."

Dawson turned to face Jenny-O who slathered gray costume makeup onto his cheeks. We were supposed to be zombies. *Not very good ones*, I thought.

"Whatever, man," I snapped. "My parents are just a little protective, okay?"

"Protective? Your mom still believes in that 4th street candy story *and* makes you do the Safe Candy thing at the hospital!"

M.M. let himself through the side fence and appeared just in time to hear Jenny-O's comment. "Yeah, we ain't doing that, bro. screw that," he said as he took the joint I offered. He exhaled onto my face, the cold air and his breath making it billow like white smoke. I swatted it away.

"No candy checks, guys. I'm totally cool this year, remember? No parental involvement."

Ever since I could remember my mom made me take my candy to the hospital to be X-rayed after trick-or-treating. It was that stupid 4th street urban legend. Wasn't she too old for that crap? Like a million years ago some little girl got a bad piece of candy, like a tack in it or something, and the hospital started the Safe Candy program. For free you take the candy and they X-ray it to make no crazy person stuck something in them.

What about poison, I always thought. *They can't see that with an X-ray.*

The idea of it still scared me, but not enough that I'd make an idiot out of myself in front of my friends and be the killjoy who said no.

They dropped the subject and we finished our makeup.

* * *

Three hours later our pillowcases were bulging with hundreds of candies, and even some full sized items. Without younger siblings slowing us down, our haul was huge. We hit every neighborhood within walking distance.

Including the scattering of houses on 4th street. I don't know what my mom was talking about. It wasn't scary in the day or night. Everyone was nice when they opened the door—old people mostly—and gave us huge handfuls of candy. I was glad my friends pushed me to go down there with them. There wasn't anything to be afraid of.

It was a half hour before my curfew. We were settled inside the lower level of a jungle gym at the elementary school playground gorging ourselves, trading out any candy from our hauls we didn't like. M.M. and Jenny-O were making out in the section beside us. I hadn't looked over in a while since it grossed me out, but since they'd been quiet I guessed they were still going at it.

"I love trick-or-treating. Why would we ever stop going? I mean, people handing out free candy? Freakin' awesome. I'll never get too old for this." Dawson tore open two mini-Snickers, popping both in his mouth and chewing obnoxiously.

And that's when it all went wrong. That's when I knew that Candy Check stuff my mom laid into me about was true.

The Butterfinger looked fine when I unwrapped it—*did I even look at it?*—so the pain that went through me when I chewed was a horrifying surprise. As I bit down on it the razorblade—*that had to be it, I know that's what it is*—slid between the gap of my canine and molar. The force of my jaw wedged the shard of metal up hard and fast. Coppery, hot blood flooded my mouth in an instant.

"Hey, man, stop kidding around. I—"

Dawson started foaming at the mouth, his words cut short. Thick globs of spit dripped down his chin. The streetlights cast enough of an amber glow in the confined space to reveal his eyes rolling back into his head.

He tried standing but swayed, tripping over the divider between our section and Jenny-O and M.M.'s. Dawson fell onto them, his body convulsing violently.

My head turned, finally looking into the other room. When Jenny-O and M.M. didn't move or yell as Dawson choked on his own fluids, thrashing around like a water-deprived fish, I knew they must be dead from whatever nightmare their candy had been laced with.

I couldn't move—*so much blood*—or do anything but sit flat on my ass, bleeding from the razor lodged in my gums and stare at my friends' dead bodies.

Shock. I'm in shock.

"Help," I tried to yell, but the wave of liquid that spewed from my mouth turned the plea into a soft gurgle.

I wished my mom or dad went with me, or told me I couldn't go alone for one more year. I wished my twin brothers were there because if they had been, we'd have only been out for an hour in the neighborhood around my house.

Most of all I wished...

I wish I'd checked my candy.

Eloise J. Knapp currently resides in Washington state where her first novel (The Undead Situation) is based, working on a degree in graphic design.

Lighthouse
By Benny Alano

Most of us know what lighthouses are and what they are there for, right? We know that a lighthouse shoots a beam of light across the coast so ships know when they are about to reach land. This is common knowledge, correct? Well what if I told you that this is not the real reason why we have lighthouses? What if this was only half true?

It all started on a gloomy October night. A lighthouse operator by the name of Joseph Green was sitting at the top of the lighthouse working the night shift. There wasn't much work for him to do; everything was automated and Joseph always spent his nights wondering why he was there.

Hours dragged by as Joseph stared out into the sea, listening to the ship horns blaring. The ship's captain would do this to signal the lighthouse operator, a way to tell him thanks for the warning. The seas are pitch black at night, so if the lighthouse was not there, ships would surly crash into land.

The night continued and Joseph began to drift into a sleep. He shook it off and stood from the command chair. A cot was set up in that same room for him to sleep on. He lay on the cot and quickly closed his eyes.

An hour passed since Joseph fell asleep. It was then that a loud beeping began. His eyes flashed open, but all he could see was black. The oversized light bulb had burnt out. His training began to run through his mind. He knew where the extra bulbs were and knew how to change it, but for some reason he couldn't move.

Moaning and cries of pain began to drift into the air. Chills ran down his back as he listened. A loud ship horn blared, overpowering the ghostly moans. He snapped out of it and darted out of the bed. *I need to get the light back on to warn the ship,* he thought. In one of the drawers there was a flashlight. He fumbled his way toward it. The small beam of light pierced the darkness and he was now able to see a little.

The moans continued.

He peered down toward the shoreline and there, he saw them. Hundreds upon hundreds of ghostly white figures were shambling out of the water and up the shoreline. Joseph froze. They continued to whine in a gargled tone as if they had water in their lungs. The ghosts were walking toward a collection of beach houses just across the street.

A ships horn blared again snapping him back to reality. He needed to get that light back up and running. He ran down to the storage containers and grabbed a new bulb. He ran back and started climbing the latter to the light. Changing the light bulb was practically the same as changing one in a house. This one is just bigger. He snapped the new bulb into place and climbed down. He rebooted the control panel and the new bulb sparkled to life.

Joseph peered down to the shoreline again and saw the ghost turn away from the houses and began dissipating back into the water. He stared as the last one disappeared.

The radio began to squawk, startling Joseph. He reached for the microphone and began talking, "Light keeper."

"Glad you got the light up and running again. This was a close one," a voice answered.

Joseph stood there puzzled; he didn't quite understand what the man was talking about. "What do you mean by 'close one'?"

"Don't you know?"

"No."

"The lighthouse isn't just so ships can know where the coast line is. It's there to keep the sailors who died at sea, in the sea."

It was then that Joseph understood why he was there. "What would have happened if the ghosts reached the houses?"

"You don't wanna know," the voice replied then squawked off.

'Til this very day, no one, other than the voice at the other end of the radio, knows what would happen if the lighthouse goes out and the ghosts reach the houses.

Benny Alano *is the author of many middle grade books. His first two books* Hand Puppet Horror *and* Attack of the Vampire Snowmen *are available through Amazon.com.* www.BennyAlano.com
Email: BennyAlano@yahoo.com

Bloody Bones
By Diandra Linnemann

Gregory was prepared. He had put as many lines of defense between those pesky kids and himself as he could think of. The gate in the fence had been blocked, all windows were dark, he had put up no single decoration – and in case anyone was stupid enough to ignore these signs, there were dog poop piles scattered over the path leading up to the house. He had taken an afternoon off just to collect them.

He really *hated* Halloween!

The mechanical laughter of an unconvincing skeleton drifted over from the neighbors' place, and Gregory sighed in frustration. Obviously they had ignored his letter of complaints two weeks ago, in which he had stated how much the annual ruckus annoyed him and that they were surely breaking several laws by doing so, and that he would send over the cops if he heard anything from them that night. He had already called the cops two hours ago when the neighbors had had some kind of get-together in their front garden, which was decorated to mimic a graveyard, and there had been lots of screams and laughter. Well, it seemed the police had not deemed it necessary to make an appearance. He would have to write an explicit letter to the newspapers.

He slumped his tall frame into the old worn armchair in front of the TV and grabbed the remote. To avoid the dreadful horror movie marathons, he had tivoed several football games for the occasion. Of course he knew the results already, but it was not about the scores for him – it was about the rules, and the competition, and the way things were supposed to be.

His dinner had cooled down too much to be enjoyed while he was listening for noise from the neighbors, and he got back up to put the plate into the microwave oven. There was nothing nastier than cold mac'n'cheese. Except for candied apples, maybe. While he was waiting for the *ping!*, he drank a glass of water from the tap and stared out of the window.

Tiny shapes were running up and down the streets, screaming and laughing. With help from the street lights, he could make out several ghosts – what uncreative mother would let their kids go out like that, just put a sheet over them and be done? – a few boring classical Count Draculas and someone who had wrapped himself in old bandages to be a mummy. There were quite a number of loose ends fluttering about in the chill breeze. Some children were accompanied by their reluctant teenage siblings or by grown-ups who tried to remain as invisible as possible, to give the kids the illusion they were alone and "in charge."

As far as Gregory could remember, there was no event that could have led to his dislike of Halloween. Many friends and colleagues had asked about it, years ago, when they had still regularly tried to break down his defense and invited him to office parties, scary parties, ghost-themed parties and other nonsense. He had simply never liked the idea of Halloween. It seemed... phony. He had even, for a very brief episode as a twenty-something trying to impress the girls, immersed himself in the history of Halloween, but not even the fact that, obviously, ancient Celts had believed this to be the night when the dead returned to be merry with their families had been enough to get him to enjoy the whole mess.

PING!

Gregory sighed, retrieved his dinner from the microwave and grabbed a beer from the six-pack standing on the countertop. He did not like cold beer. In the living room, the football game was waiting for him. All he had to do was sit down and –

Somebody knocked on the door.

"Go away!" Gregory yelled, standing in the hallway, mac'n'cheese in hand.

Another knock.

Gregory sighed with frustration. He set down his plate and the beer on a small stand and headed for the door. He'd give them a piece of his mind, for sure! Drawing a deep breath, he mentally prepared to start shouting, grabbed the doorknob and pulled on it...

... and the thing in front of his door stopped him dead in his tracks.

It was tall, at least ten feet, and shaped like a human, in an oddly non-human way. Its extremities were twisted, and starved, and unbelievably long. Tiny rivers of blood were running down what was supposed to be its face, and the membrane on its head pulsed with a slow, mesmerizing rhythm.

Gregory froze to his spot. The breath he had taken refused to leave his lungs, threatening to burst his chest. He felt his hands go cold.

"You... are... bad... child." The thing had a voice, and it was deep and raw and sounded as if it was hardly ever used. It reached out and, carefully, touched Gregory's stubbled chin.

This brought him back to life. "You must have the wrong house. No children here." And he tried to close the door, but the creature's arm was in the way.

"No..." Carefully, the thing twisted itself through the narrow space between the door and doorframe. Its legs bent in improbably places, enabling it to enter the house. It left dark footprints on the cream-colored carpet. A gut-wrenching stench hovered around it and started to wrap itself around Gregory as well.

The stench made him gag and woke him from his terror-induced paralysis. "Get out of my house!"

"Is... not very... nice", the thing hissed. "Bad... boy!" It carefully touched Greg's shoulder with a long finger that ended in a ragged talon.

A shooting pain raced down his arm, and the man stared in horror as his arm, and hand, withered before his eyes. His skin turned gray, the muscles shrunk, and the pain forced him down on his knees. "Stop it!"

"Say... please." The thing smiled and revealed sharp, yellowish teeth, which stood between his lips like old gravestones in an abandoned graveyard. It started to hum a tune that sounded like a lullaby, and at the same time very, very wrong. With twisted grace it bent down and, once again, touched Gregory, the leg this time, and its touch ate his strength. The blood rivers on its head started to swell, and the membrane on its head pulsed faster.

Gregory felt his chest tighten, and his heart grow cold. "Who - who are you?" he stammered. The strength leaked from his body, and urine ran down the inside of his leg. He briefly thought about the stain this would leave on the carpet, and then surrendered to the realization that this would not matter to him. He would be gone.

The thing, while smiling its graveyard smile and gently rocking back and forth, touched his side and sang under its breath, with an unmelodic voice. "Rawhead has come out to play, out to play..." It appeared to operate with great care, so as not to damage anything, and moved with strained grace. Gregory's flesh shrank under its touch, and finally it touched just below his maxilla, and it was almost with relief that he felt the dying muscles constrict his throat. His vision blurred, and he fell over onto his side. As he faded, he still heard the creature sing. "Rawhead has come out to play..."

Diandra Linnemann, *born 1982, is a translator and writer and shares a flat with her two weird cats, a boyfriend and about a dozen dying plants. If she isn't writing, she likes to run, cook and go out for sushi with friends. She has published German and English stories in several anthologies and magazines and can be found and read online at http://shortstoriesandmadrants.blogspot.com.*

Wail
By Kate Jonez

Sunlight trickled through the lacy leaves and splashed onto Lorena's blanket. She gathered up the remains of Kit's lunch and stuffed it in the picnic basket.

"Can I go swimming yet?" the little girl called out.

Lorena stood up. Impressions of her feet in the soft moss marked her path down to the river.

"What are you building?" Lorena studied the pile of sticks bound together with vines. "Is that a castle?"

Kit nodded. She wrapped a vine around and around a stick. "This is the castle door." She wedged her creation into place. "If I had a pulley, I could make it go up and down. But I don't, so the princess will just have to open it herself."

"Are you going to be a princess when you grow up?"

"There's no such thing, Lorena." Kit rolled her eyes. "Just in fairy tales."

Lorena laughed even though she forced her face into a stern expression. "I've told you not to call me by my name. It's not polite."

"Your friends call you Lorena." Kit grinned a mischievous grin. "Aren't we friends?"

"That's enough. It's not polite."

A breeze rustled the leaves as a car passed by. Lorena's heartbeat quickened. The car was maroon, not red. It was the wrong year, wrong make, wrong model. The car sped away.

"When is Dad coming?" Kit jumped to her feet. "He promised he would come with us."

"He'll be here." Lorena's stomach clenched just like it did when she told a lie.

"Can I go swimming, yet?" Kit bounced up and down. "Those kids are." She pointed to a gaggle of splashing children in the river. They batted a red ball over their heads.

Lorena sighed. "Alright. Go on."

"Yesss!" Kit bolted for the water. She jumped in and splashed her way to the children. The red ball floated through the cerulean sky to her. She hit it back.

Lorena breathed in the mushroom damp air of the woods as she climbed back to the blanket. Maybe later they could poke around under the canopy of trees and find new flowers to press in the pages of the encyclopedia.

A shower of gravel rolled down the hill as a sporty red car skidded to a stop. A man stepped out of the car and posed like the Colossus of Rhodes with his arm shading his brow. Like a crack of thunder from an unexpected storm, the passenger door slammed shut. Franklin held out his hand to the willowy woman who wore her custom-made clothes with the casual air of a princess dressed in finery.

Lorena's stomach twisted and folded in on itself. He wouldn't dare bring that woman here. He wouldn't dare. Hatred, insistent as a cigarette burn, spread inside her. Lorena didn't move. She didn't call out. The hatred burned and blazed bigger.

Franklin squinted into the sun. He scanned left then right.

Lorena didn't move.

Finally, the princess tugged on his arm. Together, they got into the car. A shower of gravel trickled down the hill as they drove away.

"Hey lady," a boy called out. He pointed. "That guy is bothering _"

Kit screamed. She thrashed and kicked as a hulk of a man plucked her from the water and tossed her over his shoulder.

"Kit!" Lorena shrieked. Her feet furrowed up chunks of moss as she slid and scrambled down the bank

"Mom!" Kit howled. Her cries grew weaker as the man ran with her into the tangle of ferns and juniper.

Lorena rushed into the woods. Sticky pine branches snatched at her hair and blackberry spines clawed her skin. Her heart throbbed. She pushed her legs one after the other. She forced them to go.

She threw herself forward. She stumbled. She lurched. She scrambled and ran even though her body threatened to collapse. Her heart hammered hard enough to break bone.

Leaves rustled. Branches snapped. Sounds twisted her in their maelstrom. Torrents of noise rushed and battered and sucked at her pulling her into their eddy. She ran left, right, back again. Wrong place, wrong time, wrong way. Like rapids, panic roared in her ears. No matter how fast or how far she ran, she couldn't catch even a glimpse of Kit.

Lorena doubled over and gasped for breath.

Like a sign from heaven, a shard of sunlight cut through the thicket of trees. Lorena dove through the opening.

She blinked as the sunlight trickled down through the lacy leaves and splashed onto Kit lying on the blanket.

Lorena flew to her, fell to her knees at her side. She gathered her up – a bit, a piece, an arm, a leg, the remains of her. She held her tight. "I'll make it better," Lorena sobbed.

Lorena flew to the river's edge.

Children laughed as a red ball flew up into the cerulean sky.

Lorena waded into the river. Her feet were as heavy and as unwieldy as stone. She dragged them. She lifted them, one then the other. She snatched up a child.

These fingers, they are her fingers. These toes are her toes. Lorena ran with the pieces back to Kit.

Wrong size, wrong part, wrong child. Lorena screamed in panic and fear as she wrapped vines around and around her little girl. Time was slipping away. Her daughter was slipping away.

Lorena wailed and howled as she flew down to the river's edge. Frantically she searched. She would find her child – all the parts of her. She would make her better again.

Don't go down to the river, child,
Don't go there alone;
The sobbing woman, wet and wild,
Might claim you for her own. - La Llorona, Mexican folksong

Kate Jonez *writes dark fantasy fiction and non-fiction related to the research she does for stories. Her novel Candy House is currently under submission. In her spare time she enjoys ghost hunting, reading, traveling, taking photos and collecting things in jars. You can visit her Blog (www.KateJonez.com) about monsters and villains from around the world. Or connect with her on Twitter (www.Twitter.com/K8Jones) or Facebook www.Facebook.com/K8Jones.*

In The Dead House
By S. S. Michaels

Metallic crunch of aluminum. The sound of a crushed can bouncing off the stone wall and thunking to the floor echoes around the Dead House. Four's alphabet-long belch follows the crash. With his ghost tours over for the night, Four, the only guide allowed in the tunnels beneath the sedate city of Savannah, sits in the eight-by-ten dark stone chamber, known as the Dead House. It's his favorite hang-out. Every night after work, he sits on the cold cement autopsy table and drinks Bud Light from cans which he crushes against his simian forehead as soon as they're empty. Sometimes his buddy, Caleb, joins him. But not tonight.

Far away footsteps echo through the tunnels. Slow and fumbling footsteps, navigating the pitch black stone corridors. Four's ears strain. A rat? A hobo? He picks up the flashlight from the autopsy table and shines it up the steep staircase, leading to the exit.

Nothing.

He swings the bluish-white beam to the mouth of the tunnel on the opposite side of the room. He doesn't see anything, but he knows that's where the sound is coming from. He doesn't know what to do. A film of cold sweat squeezes him like a wetsuit.

A keening whine pierces the darkness.

Four scrambles toward the staircase. He drops the flashlight, catches his hip on the concrete table scrabbling his hands across the slab. His boots slide out from underneath him on the wet and mossy stones. He grimaces in pain, holding his hip, and hears someone yell for help. The flashlight. His hands grope around the black void beneath his dampened Civil War costume pants. He pulls himself up and shines his flashlight down the hall again.

A kid clings to the wall, face pressed against it, eyes squeezed shut, right hand feeling the stones in front of him. He's crying and screaming.

After nearly shitting his britches, Four rushes over to him and grabs his hand. The kid screams and recoils from Four's touch.

"Hey," Four says, "open your eyes. It's okay, I'm not a ghost or a junkie or anything."

The kid opens his eyes, squinting into Four's flashlight. He holds up a hand in front of his face, shielding his wet and running eyes.

"Sorry," Four says, pointing his flashlight over the kid's slight shoulder, peeking down the dark tunnel. "What the hell were you doing down there?"

The kid wipes a glob of translucent snot on his bare forearm. He can't be more than fourteen, fifteen years-old.

"I- I- I was on your tour, and I kind of got lost," he says, hitching and sobbing. The kid did look kind of familiar. "Something touched me back there. On the back of the neck."

"Is that why you screamed? Was that you?"

"Yeah. Wouldn't you scream if something down here touched you?" The kid jams the heels of his hands into his eye sockets, desperate to wipe away the tears.

Four shines his flashlight down the tunnel, sweeping the beam back and forth. "It was probably a spider web or something. See 'em all hanging from the ceiling?" Reminiscent of the Spanish moss that decorates the live oaks above them, cob webs and spider webs hang from the ten foot ceiling, caught in the beam of light. Four snorts out a laugh. "Sometimes they fall, that's all. No biggie." He smiles at the kid who does his best to smile back and force out a wet laugh. Four leads the kid up the steep flight of stairs to the heavy iron door and releases him out into the soft illumination of Forsyth Park.

"Kids," Four says with a huff. He descends again, lays on the cold slab and cracks another beer. The watery barley taste floods his mouth and cascades down his esophagus, loosening his muscles.

He shuts off his flashlight and stares at the gray skylight eight feet up.

He wonders what it would be like to be dead.

Or no, worse, dying in this place. Lots of people, mostly soldiers, came down here to die and then be sliced up after they passed of yellow fever. That was back in the 1800s. A rare chill touches Four's spine.

A slight skittering sound touches his ears.

He sits up.

He doesn't hear it again.

He lies back down.

A slithering, dragging sound catches his ear.

This time he sits up and grabs the flashlight, turning it again down the tunnel. Its bright beam wavers. He shakes the flashlight and smacks it against his palm. The light flickers.

And everything goes black.

"Shit," Four mutters, knocking his beer on the floor with a liquid thud. He shakes the flashlight and it comes on.

He aims it at the tunnel and it winks out again.

"Fuck."

He hears the slithering/dragging again.

Probably a rat. Maybe a snake. Ew, don't think about that. It's nothing.

He cracks another beer. One for the road.

He reclines on the cold hard slab again, humming some Lynyrd Skynyrd tune.

He doesn't see the shroud-wrapped figure crouching by the built-in sink, a foot from his fat head.

S. S. Michaels *is a writer of transgressive fiction, with several novels on submission and two anthologies in the works. She has lived abroad, traveled widely, jumped out of an airplane and driven a race car. She has worked in film and television for such organizations as Ridley Scott's Scott Free, dick clark productions, inc., and CBS. She lives on the Georgia coast with her husband, two kids, two dogs, and a swarm of unfriendly sand gnats.*

The Monster Under my Bed
By Bryan Medof

My mommy kissed me on my forehead and turned out the light. She shut my bedroom door leaving a vertical ring of light around it, but that wasn't enough light to console me. The dim glow from a Minnie Mouse nightlight across my room was my only comfort from this suffocating darkness.

I brought the covers up to my chin and I was as careful as I could, because I dared not to dangle my hand or leg off the bed –for fear that the monster living underneath it will grab me.

Every night since I got my own room, I've dreaded this time, bedtime. I tried telling mommy and daddy about the monster, but they don't believe me. They just tell me that it is all in my imagination and that, monsters are *not* real; but I know that they are, because I've heard one – I've heard the one that lives under my bed, and it *wants* me. As long as I don't get up for anything, like something to drink or eat, or use the bathroom, I'll be safe.

But as each night passes by, the monster seems to be getting more hostile.

I'm so scared, I lie here staring at my nightlight until my eyes become heavy, but this night, the sounds of a hissing breath beneath me keeps me awake. It slowly calls out my name in a whispery tone:

"Cin-dy . . . I have . . . something . . . for . . . you . . ."

I pretend not to hear its creepy, rustling voice, but I know it knows that I heard it. It can hear my heart beating against my chest and my own breathing growing heavier.

"Cin-dy. . . come . . . here . . . I . . . have . . . some-thing . . . for you . . ."

I looked back at my nightlight, and then I noticed something strange in the mirror transfixed to my dresser, something quivering.

It was the monster!

Oh God, help me! I feel my face distorting uncontrollably in fear. Its glowing eyes radiated a red luminescence glare from under my bed. I suddenly felt hot, as if its eyes were producing heat.

"Cin-dy . . . I . . . need . . . some-thing . . . from . . . you."

It was then that I finally realized that if I could see it, then it could *see* me. Oh why is this happening to me? I quickly pulled the covers over my head to hide.

As a few moments passed, my bed began to shake a little, but I couldn't tell if it was my own shivering or the monster growing restless.

"Please leave me alone." I pleaded, hoping it will respect my wish.

"Come . . . down . . . here . . . first."

"No," I said. "Leave me alone, please."

"Don't . . . make . . . me . . . come . . . GET – YOU!"

Then I heard a creak from the floor near my bedroom door.

"Mommy!"

But no answer . . .

"Mommy!" I yelled a little louder.

The doorknob turned and the door opened. And for a moment I felt relieved when I saw my mommy as she walked in, "Honey, did you call me?"

"Yes," I cried. "The monster, it's under my bed."

Mommy took a deep breath in frustration, "Now Cindy, I'm really getting tired of this, there are no such thing as monsters."

"But I swear –"

"Stop it, now go to sleep."

"But it's under my bed right now, I'm not lying!"

But before I could saying anything more, she stormed to my bed and angrily bent down, flinging the lower covers onto my bed. I quickly sat up and looked down at her as she tilted her head.

"Now see, there is nothing under your –"

Suddenly, a hand burst out like a rattlesnake attacking its prey, the skin was reptilian in texture and appeared slimy as the slivers of light danced off its ghoulish surface, and it grabbed my mommy by her wrist and yanked her under my bed with such a thrust that it literally lifted my bed from off the ground.

She screamed in horror and I could tell she was in great agony, I could her it ripping her flesh off of her body, the horrible sound reminded me of the bubbly suction noise from a shoe lifting out of the mud.

I screamed, and tears finally began to pour from my eyes. Daddy ran to my room and turned on the light and saw me sitting up in bed in shock, my eyes as wide as the full moon above, and a puddle of blood oozing out from under my bed.

"What in the hell?" he said, his voice was quivering and broken.

When he looked back at me, I raised my arms up, hoping that he would grab me and save me, but then the power went out and all I heard was the raging roar of the monster and the fading screams of daddy as he too was dragged under my bed.

Now, in the complete darkness of the night, I lay in the center of my bed wide-awake, and I wait. I wait till morning, for the only light that can keep the monster at bay now, the sunlight.

And while I wait in dread, the monster continues to whisper my name . . .

Bryan Medof *lives in Riverside, California. He is an aspiring artist, specializing in oil and acrylics, a classical pianist, composer and periodically teaches the piano and music theory. Bryan is currently writing a novel. His other interest other than the arts: philosophy, forensic psychology, astronomy, world history and ancient mythology.*

Thirteen
By Joe Dibuduo & Kate Robinson

"There will be no Halloween activities this year. We'll treat the day the same as any other," Mrs. Olsen said.

Everyone in the 7th grade English class groaned. Steven turned to Hannah, who sat beside him. "What does she have against celebrating Halloween?"

"You weren't here last year, were you?" Hannah said.

"You know I only got here a month ago."

"Oh yeah, sorry," Hannah said, thinking about how much she should tell him.

"You going to tell me, or what?"

"Sure, okay . . . On Halloween last year, Hank and Marvin rigged up a holographic image projector."

"A what?" Steven looked at Hannah with wide eyes.

"Something Marvin's father used in the Gulf War to fool the Iraqis into thinking they were shooting at his jet. They were actually shooting at a holographic image he projected onto the sky. It's a three-dimensional image that looks real."

"No way. Stuff like that is science fiction."

"Yeah, tell that to the soldiers who wasted all their ammo shooting at holograms."

"I don't believe it," Steven said.

"Marvin's dad said it provided a distraction while he bombed his target. Then he showed Marvin how holographic projectors worked," Hannah said.

"Yeah sure, he had one sitting in his living room," Steven said.

"No, it was in his basement," Hannah said.

"You're lying."

"No, I swear, I'm telling you like it is."

"Okay, so tell me. What did they do with this holographic thing?"

"Well, last year, Mrs. Olsen organized the Halloween party. She gathered the entire school in the auditorium to plan it . . ."

Hannah cleared her throat and started talking like Mrs. Olsen, who always tried to be spooky in her prim, proper, teacher's voice

"She said something like this - there's *no* better place to celebrate Halloween than around a bonfire to keep away the *chill* on a *dark, spooky* night. The moon will be *full* and will bring *ghosts, goblins,* and *witches!* We'll also use the bonfire to *cast away* our worries. Write down any aspect of your life that you want to *disappear.* Toss the paper *into* the bonfire and *imagine* that worry *vanishing.* If it does *disappear,* credit the power of *positive* thinking for your success! There's *no* such thing as magic! Or *is* there? Be sure to dress *warm* and meet me on the soccer field at 8 p.m. to find out!"

"Ha, I can't imagine Mrs. Olsen being awake at 8 p.m."

Hannah giggled. "Oh, she was awake, all right."

Steven squirmed in his seat. "Well, come on, tell me what happened!"

"Marvin had a brainstorm and recruited Hank to help him."

"Okay, I'll bite. Help him with what?"

Hannah smiled. "Marvin made this video with twelve witches flying on brooms, and then asked his dad to make a hologram out of it. He practiced making the three-dimensional images appear all over his basement. When he heard about the bonfire, he figured he could cast the images in the night sky. He and Hank set up the projector in a schoolroom by the soccer field. Then they put wireless speakers in trees around the field."

"That was clever," Steven said. "So what happened next?"

"Well, Marvin knew there'd be a harvest moon that night."

"What's a harvest moon?"

"It's the full moon nearest to the autumnal equinox."

Steven rolled his eyes. "I'm not going to ask what *that* is. So what about the moon?"

Hannah smiled again. "Marvin figured it would be a great backdrop for his flying witches. He and Hank got everything ready, turned the sound down so they could practice without being noticed, and projected one witch. The holographic image looked real, as though it really flew across the moon. If they didn't know better, they would have believed what they saw."

"Cool," Steven said, "I bet they couldn't wait."

"They waited until the right time."

"Come on, tell me what happened."

"Three hundred kids and their teachers crowded onto the field and Mrs. Olsen lit a roaring bonfire. Everyone wrote out the negative things they wanted to change in their lives and marched by the bonfire, throwing their scraps of paper in it, hoping to make their worries vanish as the ashes floated to the sky . . ."

* * *

Marvin and Hank watched from the shadows until the field filled up. Just before Mrs. Olsen started to speak, Hank whispered, "Now's the time."

Marvin started the projector and Hank snapped the sound system on. A horrendous shriek startled everyone on the field. Cackles followed the scream. Heads turned, groups gathered together in fear. Some girls hugged each other. Everyone looked for the source. One kid pointed at the moon and yelled, "Witches!"

Silhouetted against a full harvest moon on their brooms, a dozen cackling holographic figures flew through the night sky, looking like they intended to employ their magic on everyone below. The kids gaped at the black hats and flowing robes of the hideous-looking women as they skimmed in around in startling maneuvers across the sky. Then students and teachers alike made a mad dash for the school.

Marvin and Hank rolled on the ground laughing until Marvin counted the images and found there were now thirteen instead of a dozen.

"Something's wrong," he shouted. "There can't be thirteen. I only made twelve."

Hank shivered. "Is there something wrong with the machine?"

Marvin checked the projector. "It's only projecting twelve. What the – how could there be thirteen?" He stared up at the cackling witches and counted them again. Thirteen. Goosebumps rose all over his arms. He bent over the projector and tried to fix it so there were only twelve.

Hank jumped up just in time to see the witch speeding toward their room. "Holy Moly, that one's flying at supersonic speed . . . look out, she's headed right for us!"

An ear-splitting scream sprang from the witch as she crashed through the solid wall like a ghost. "You boys fooled me tonight! I thought by joining the group I made number thirteen! For your dirty deed, I'm going to make you pay. I know you're only boys and don't know any better, so I'll turn you into girls. From now on you'll know better than to mess with a witch."

Marvin and Hank tried to scramble out the door.

"Molasses fill the air, catch the boys in your goo," she shouted, casting a spell.

Both boys struggled in a sudden mass of sticky gel. The witch cackled with glee.

"Tell you what boys, if you don't want to be girls, you can accompany me to the Monsters Ball. If you're good, I may forego the gender change."

The boys looked at each other like they'd better obey. "Before we go, what's that?" Marvin asked.

The witch let out another delighted cackle. "The dead shake their bones at the Monsters Ball. You'll dance with me and any other who may want to hold some living flesh instead of cold, damp bones."

Hank shuddered. "You mean we have to dance with dead people?"

"Depends what you mean by dead. Some of the dead are more alive than many with years left to live. It's all in your soul!" She flew around the room in a blur and cackled so loud that the boys had to hold their ears.

"Hop on," she said, and pointed to her broom.

"No way," both boys said together. Marvin's knees chattered and Hank's hands trembled.

"Okay, I guess you want to be girls, then." She pointed her wand at them.

Both boys jumped on her broom.

***

"How do you know all this?" Steven asked Hannah.

"I have a very close relationship with Hank," Hannah said.

"He's your boyfriend?"

"Sort of . . . it's complicated. Anyway, Marvin wrapped his arms around the ugly old witch, and Hank wrapped his arms around Marvin . . ."

***

The boys were about to protest when the broom shuddered to life and took off, headed straight toward the moon at a speed that dazzled them. "Up, up, and away! See, better than Superman!" The witch cackled at her own joke.

The boys looked down at the twelve holographic witches still flying around the field. Marvin screamed and Hank tightened his grip. It seemed the broom would really go all the way to the moon. Both shut their eyes and silently prayed the broom wouldn't do anything other than land safely. After some hair-raising minutes, a brightly lit broom landing strip came into view. They were the only multiple-occupant broom in the air, and had to circle until all the single-occupant brooms landed. All the other witches pointed and smiled their toothy grins in the boys' direction.

"Guess the witches are the same as the dead," Marvin said.

Hank trembled. "What are you talking about?"

"Hold on boys," their witch said. "Not one of us witches are dead yet, but when we are, we'll certainly show up here every year to dance."

A witch on the ground waved them in. Their heavy broom almost crash-landed, but their witch chanted an extra magic spell to stabilize it. As the boys stared around at the strange sights, she hung her broom on a long rack with hundreds of other brooms.

A mausoleum large enough to be a palace stood right next to the landing field. Around it, a graveyard extended as far as the eye could see. The dead were clawing themselves out of the ground and grooming their flesh and bones with handfuls of mud. When satisfied with their appearance, they shuffled their way to the Mausoleum Hall, where thirteen skeletons played music on their bones. The wall-to-wall dance floor was crowded with hopping and bopping, clapping and stamping, grooving and hooving creatures.

"By the way, my name is Griselda. If anyone here wants to dance with you, you can refuse by telling them you're with me."

"What will happen if we refuse and don't tell them your name?" Marvin asked.

"Simple, my boy. You'll be dancing once a year."

Marvin gulped. Beside him, a girl dressed in a pretty blue gown with a big bloodstain across the bodice took Hank by the hand. "Come waltz with me," she said.

A smile lit Hank's face at the sight of a beauty amongst the living dead. He took her by the hand. "Are you really dead?" he asked.

"Yes, it's been a week."

"Were you wearing this gown when you died?"

"I was at church for my sister's wedding. When the church bells rang, one came loose and fell on my head."

She turned and maggots crawled from the side of her head. Hank turned in revulsion, but she held him tight, pulling him close. He shut his eyes as maggots dropped from her cheek to her shoulder.

Marvin shook him by the shoulder. "Tell her what Griselda said!"

"I'm with Griselda," Hank finally managed to say.

The girl let go and grabbed a rotting hunk just walking by. Hank watched as the maggots rolled from her dress onto the floor to be squashed by the other dancers. He held his nose to shut out the stench of rotten flesh.

A witch uglier than Griselda grabbed Marvin by the hand, but he broke free. "Please, please, take me away from here. I promise never to mess with a witch again," he begged Griselda.

"Me too," Hank said.

A look of disappointment washed over Griselda's face as she checked her broom from the rack. The trio surged into the sky and headed home.

Griselda took them back to the school grounds. "Sorry boys, I'm going to have to turn you into girls."

"No, no. . . please," they begged.

* * *

"When they ran into the bathroom and looked into the mirror, they saw . . ." Hannah said, grinning.

Steven made a face. "Quite a story, but you don't really expect me to believe that, do you?"

"Believe what you want, but at this time last year, my name was Hank," Hannah said. Ask anybody."

Steven crossed his arms. "I'll *never* believe it."

Hannah started laughing. Her features began to change and in a deeper voice she said, "Thank you, Steven... er, I better call you Stephanie from now on."

"That's not funny." Steven put his hands to his mouth in a gesture of surprise because his voice sounded much higher than usual.

"Griselda told me the only way to change back is to find a boy and tell him this story on Halloween. If he doesn't believe the story, he'd become a girl and I'd change back into a boy," Hank said.

"But I don't want to be a girl," Stephanie wailed. "I believe, I believe, now change me back."

"It's not that easy," Hank said.

"*I don't care how hard it is!*" Stephanie shouted in her now shrill voice. "What do I have to do? I can't go through life as a, a . . . *girl*!"

"Stephanie, you'll have to find a boy to listen to your story. And this is important – you have to tell the story on Halloween, or it won't work."

"But today *is* Halloween."

"Hurry up then," Hank said, "or you'll either be dancing at the mausoleum or end up wearing dresses for at least a year!"

Joe DiBuduo and Kate Robinson used to attend the same crit group and decided to have some fun telecommuting between Arizona and California to create short fiction for kids and adults. DiBuduo sports a vivid imagination and Robinson wields the toolbox and the word-whacking polish.

HALLOWEEN

A YOUNG READER'S BOOK ABOUT SPELLS, FRIENDSHIP, AND PUPPETS THAT COME TO LIFE!

When Jays hand puppet, Yeti Booger, comes to life and defends him against Greg, the school bully, he thinks its the coolest thing in the world. After the creature becomes more than he can handle, Jay must figure out how Yeti Booger came to life and stop him before anyone else is hurt. It truly is a HAND PUPPET HORROR.

Hand Puppet HORROR
https://www.createspace.com/3568570
ISBN/EAN13: 1460938917 / 9781460938911

Also Available on Amazon.com and at Barnes & Noble

Benny Alano is the author of many scary children and middle grade books. He lives in Southern California with his wife and daughter. Benny loves hearing from kids who read his books. You can contact him by emailing: BennyAlano@yahoo.com

Or follow him on Twitter: http://www.Twitter.com/BennyAlano

A YOUNG READER'S BOOK ABOUT VAMPIRES, ZOMBIES, DARK MAGIC AND A SANTA CLAUS THAT CAN KICK BUTT!

Attack of the VAMPIRE Snowmen

Written by Benny Alano Illustrated by Jessica Geis

With only a few days before the big night, Santa Claus is kidnapped by an army of vampire snowmen; it's up to Laidenn, Claus' only dark elf-in-training, to enlist the help of the living dead elves to defeat the snowmen and bring Claus back.

Attack of the VAMPIRE Snowmen
https://www.createspace.com/3574908
ISBN/EAN13: 1460973518 / 9781460973516

Also Available on Amazon.com and at Barnes & Noble

Benny Alano is the author of many scary children and middle grade books. He lives in Southern California with his wife and daughter. Benny loves hearing from kids who read his books. You can contact him by emailing: BennyAlano@yahoo.com

Or follow him on Twitter: http://www.Twitter.com/BennyAlano

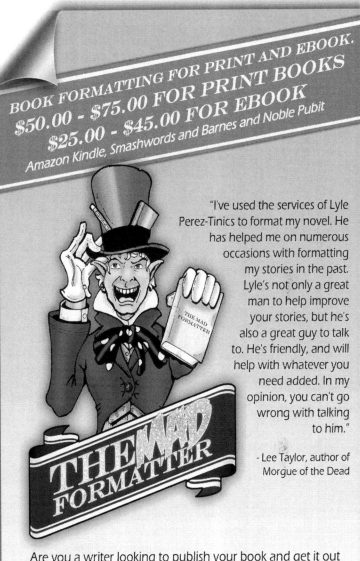

BOOK FORMATTING FOR PRINT AND EBOOK.
$50.00 - $75.00 FOR PRINT BOOKS
$25.00 - $45.00 FOR EBOOK
Amazon Kindle, Smashwords and Barnes and Noble Pubit

"I've used the services of Lyle Perez-Tinics to format my novel. He has helped me on numerous occasions with formatting my stories in the past. Lyle's not only a great man to help improve your stories, but he's also a great guy to talk to. He's friendly, and will help with whatever you need added. In my opinion, you can't go wrong with talking to him."

- Lee Taylor, author of Morgue of the Dead

Are you a writer looking to publish your book and get it out there? Do you want to make your manuscript shine? Take a look at my service and let me help make your book interior exceptional. We all know that Word can be a pain sometimes, so let The Mad Formatter help you!

www.themadformatter.com

coming soon from KnightWatch Press

 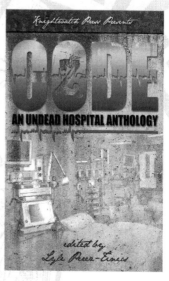

Mark Bliss has spent most of his adult life working at a pawnshop. For years, he has ripped people off with no remorse. That is until the day an elderly woman named Maggie Bliss, walks in through the door and brings an army of living dead with her. DEMENT is a story that truly lives up to its title. Join Mark as he slowly goes insane on the roof of a pawnshop, while the bodies of the dead linger below.

We all know many of the best Zombie flicks and books make their start in or around a hospital but they soon leave the confines of the medical building and start to lay waste to the world but what happens in those first few hours.
" CODE Z - An Undead Hospital Anthology " is a horror anthology with an undead theme. Tales of life excitement and of course the undead. Each story is unique and new.

www.knightwatchpress.info

Made in the USA
Middletown, DE
15 September 2015